T0191180

God's Country

Other Books by
Percival Everett

God's Country

A NOVEL

Percival Everett

Beacon Press
BOSTON

BEACON PRESS
Boston, Massachusetts
www.beacon.org

Beacon Press books
are published under the auspices of
the Unitarian Universalist Association of Congregations.

27 26 25 24   8 7 6 5 4 3 2

This book is printed on acid-free paper that meets the uncoated paper
ANSI/NISO specifications for permanence as revised in 1992.

Library of Congress Cataloging-in-Publication Data is available for this title
ISBN 978-0-8070-1629-9 (acid-free paper)
Ebook ISBN 978-0-8070-1630-5

For my Chessie, always, forever

Introduction
Madison Smartt Bell

PERCIVAL EVERETT'S THIRD NOVEL, *Cutting Lisa*, came to me in the mail in London, with a note from our mutual editor, Cork Smith—addressed to Percival Everett. I'd accidentally received the author's first copy of the book. Because of the cost of international mail I sent back only a note describing the mistake. I kept the novel and read it with a growing admiration. The story of a doctor who, for truly inevitable reasons, performs an abortion on his own daughter-in-law, *Cutting Lisa* is quick, efficient, ruthless. When I turned the last page I found the author photo and thought, before I could stop myself, *Oh, did it say somewhere those characters are black?*

Well, as a matter of fact it didn't. I read it again to be sure. *Cutting Lisa* doesn't mention what color the characters are. It isn't an issue. They are just people. Race doesn't come into it at all.

Race does come into *God's Country*, mainly because his whiteness is the best claim the narrator, Curt Marder, has to a right to exist. *God's Country* is Everett's second Western. The first, *Walk Me to the Distance*, is as starkly realistic as *Cutting Lisa*. Its narrator is a black man in a landscape where there aren't any others (not many people of any description, actually), and because his color isn't a consuming subject for him the reader doesn't hear much about it either; in *Walk Me to the Distance*, race is not an issue. But race, and every other kind of arbitrary social distinction, are always much on the mind of Curt Marder in *God's Country*, because he'd have no claim to any worth at all on his own merits.

The device of placing a no-count rogue in a well-known historical setting has been perfected by George MacDonald Fraser, but Marder has none of the scurvy charm of Fraser's Flashman. What makes him comic is his obliviousness. Everett's realistic fiction is always about taxingly difficult moral choices; *God's Country*, a satire, presents those sorts of choices too, but Marder unfailingly makes the very worst of them, and usually without realizing that there's a choice to consider. And that, we begin to see as the story unfolds, is Everett's bitterly ironic vision of How the West Was Won—by numberless versions of Marder making all their decisions out of the most narrowly circumscribed self-interest imaginable, and all in the unexamined belief that something like manifest destiny will carry them to the exalted level they believe to be theirs. Asked, toward the end, if he has "any dreams," Marder says, "I want me a lot of money and to be able to tell folks what to do and to have me a nice, big spread and to have my name mean somethin'."

In his reality, Marder can't tell hardly anybody what to do; grown white folks all despise him, and he has trouble making much of an impression even on small children. The only person he can pretend to boss around is Bubba, the black tracker he has hired (though without capacity to pay him) to lead him through the Swiftian convolutions of the plot. Bubba is a sort of tragic hero opposed to Marder's contemptible buffoon, but we see him as it were through the wrong end of the binoculars, because Marder has no perception at all of the moral issues and conflicts that Bubba has to negotiate. Besides, Bubba is in some ways the classic Western hero: a man of few words (as very few words are safe for him to say), of long and frequent stillnesses, and less frequently, of totally committed and decisive actions— as different from Marder as black from white, or night from day. Where Marder spends all of his time in a fog of incomprehension he can't even recognize, Bubba has the kind of clarity that may come to someone whose moves are mostly forced; his last word, nearly, is "I ain't dyin' for nobody exceptin' myself."

Don't think this book isn't funny. Even Everett's serious and realistic books have their covert strain of dark humor, and here the wit is out in the open, as agile and as cutting as Mark Twain's. Everett has the broad tonal range Twain did, so that he can convincingly move through a series of relatively light satirical flourishes to *God's Country*'s stunningly grave conclusion. But laughing at Marder is a little uncomfortable all the way through, at least for a white American. For us, laughing at Marder is like what kicking him must be for the other characters in the book. We worry he's going to stick to our shoe. We can't kick him all the way out of the picture. In the end, he's the one we have to own, not Bubba.

God's Country

1

I SAW THE SMOKE FIRST. Too much smoke to just be spilling out of the chimney, so I kicked my gray and hurried to the top of the hill. More than a cozy fire in the hearth, it was my danged house burning to beat all get out. Red and yellow flames were leaping up into the sky just under thick smoke. And around it all were men, seedy looking from a distance even, riding around screamin' and hollerin'. Two were tossing more torches to the house, two were shootin' arrows every which way into things and one had my wife hung over his saddle like a rug. She was swearin' a blue streak that made me proud, dang proud. I couldn't rightly make out the words, but the tone was right for good cussin'.

They'd shot a sticker into my poor hound and he looked damn pitiful running around in tight circles like he was caught in a twister. I had a half a mind to ride down that hill and say somethin', but it was just half a mind after all, and I didn't suspect they'd listen at that moment. There were five of them and they were high on plunder. No reachin' a soul high on plunder. It's not like I didn't do anything. I did pull my gun out of its holster and stand my ground.

They finally left with a showy and loud display of horse-braying that I felt was unnecessary and in poor taste. They rode away with my Sadie and left old Blue all red and still. I went down as the dust settled to inspect the scene. It was a mess. The house and barn, what was left of them, were sizzlin' and poppin' and the smoke made my eyes burn. They didn't leave a dang thing. Was nothing sacred? I asked the sky, "Ain't nothing sacred?" And the big, unforgivin' western sky smiled big and said nothing.

I looked at all the arrows stuck into everything and figured they had shot 'em around to make folks think Indians was to blame. I sat on the ground and wondered about it. What if they was Indians dressed like white men to cast suspicion the other way? I stood and picked up old Blue by the arrow, climbed back on my horse and started for town with Blue as proof that, regardless who they was, they was shootin' arrows.

As I rode the trail away from the smoke and ashes that had been my life, I considered the face of my Sadie. I saw it there, bouncing against the saddle of the varmint that stole her, a little fuller than when we first met, just like the whole of her I reckon, but still it was the face of my woman. Naw, it weren't the face of one of them showgirls in Dodge City what sings and dances, but it was the face I was used to waking up to, and it was thumping against some strange leather on a trail to God knew where. She was off to some horrible plight that I found generally unpleasant to consider, but that's the way life is, though, full of strange leather.

The heat was beating down on me something awful, making my hat band darken and the insides of my thighs raw as they scrubbed my saddle. My horse had slowed considerable, but there was no water to steer him toward. I nodded near fainting, slumped forward and I noticed that Blue had slipped from the arrow somewhere along the way, but it didn't matter none as I was sure people would just as soon study the sticker minus any fleshy deposit.

The town wasn't much to look at, but then it wasn't much to visit either. It had a damn embarrassing name and it pained me to tell folks I lived near it. And since this here is my story, I won't say. But there that god-forsaken collection of shacks and stables lay, and me on the gone side of heatstroke with nothing to see but its weathered planks behind a wall of heat rising from the earth that made the whole mess wiggle like in a dream. I rode through the middle of town and then fell off onto the dry, cracked ground that even sounded dusty when I hit. No one rushed to my aid and I figured such heat was bound to slow bodies down, but I was struck with a sad feeling about the way folks don't care no more about their fellow fellows. Then Terkle was standing over me, the little redheaded barkeep, and he was talking.

"Curt Marder, you no-good, free-loadin', back-slidin', dog-lipped son-of-a-mud-rat, you owe me three dollars!" was what he said.

I just looked at him and then I looked at myself, dusty and lying in the street and I told him, "Renegades burned my house."

"Three dollars and I ain't charged you a lick of interest. If I had a lick of sense, I wouldn't offer you no credit. No-siree Robert."

"Burned my barn."

"Petersen over at the general store has got a few words for you after me."

"They run off with my wife."

"You're not taking advantage of our Christian charity anymore."

"Killed my dog."

"Killed your dog?"

"With this here arrow." I held up the deadly device for him to see. "He was on the other end, but he fell off."

Terkle fell to sitting on his butt in the street. "Killed your dog?" He shook his head. "What kind of heathens do we have in these parts?"

"Efficient." I looked at the sky and saw the day was passing. "I need help."

"You just came home and found your dog stuck, eh?"

"Not exactly. I seen the vermin. I seen them shoot my dog with this here arrow and laugh whilst he run round and round in front of 'em."

"Did you shoot at 'em?"

"Well, they were out of range, you see. I had my gun drawn though and damn if they didn't ride like the wind the other way."

"Geez, Marder, I'm awful sorry I laid into you the way I did after you just watched your puppy get murdered and all," Terkle said.

"It's okay, Terk. How's a body to know something's wrong when a man's lying in the dusty road clutching a bloody arrow in his hand?"

"I suppose you're right." Terkle took a deep breath and looked at the sky. "Well, come on to the tavern and let me pour you one."

I let him help me to my feet. "That's right kind of you."

"That'll bring your tab to three dollars and ten cents."

The saloon was a dingy affair with small windows and doors that squawked miserably every time they swung. It was dusk when I got in there, and the lanterns that did work gave off a yellow light that made you feel worse than darkness. Blind Mitch, the nigger piano player, was banging away at the key that worked, playing that jig music that was hard to whistle. I leaned up against the bar next to Wide Clyde McBride. He smelled something fierce and it struck me that I probably did as well, but Christ almighty. Then Terk pushed a glass of whiskey in front of me and I figured if a man can't smell like shit in a tavern full of like-stinking men full of joy juice, then what was the country coming to. I threw back the drink and coughed into my fist.

"What happened to you?" Wide asked.

"Renegades," I said.

Terk pointed at the arrow I'd set down on the bar. "Stuck his puppy," he said.

"Heathens," Wide said.

I shook my head and tapped my glass. "That ain't the all of it," I said. "They burned my house and my barn, killed my milk cow and my best pulling mule and then run off with my Sadie, my woman, the light of my life."

Wide turned to the few other people sitting at the tables and said, "You boys hear that? The bastards killed the man's dog."

"Did you get a good look at 'em?" Wide asked. A couple of fellas who'd been playing poker came and stood beyond him at the bar.

"Can't say that I did. But they was a jovial bunch, laughing and having a big ol' time."

"Tinjuns?" one of the men asked. He was a good head

taller than Wide and had one of them harelip things, so it was hard to understand him most of the time. As far as we knew, his name was Taharry.

"They was dressed like white men, but they was shootin' arrows. Shootin' arrows this way and that and burning my house like Injuns. I don't know what they was."

Wide picked up the arrow and studied it, then passed it to the next man. They grumbled and shook their heads.

"Recognize the feather work?" I asked the lot.

"Naw."

"Nope."

"Don't know one band of heathens from the next, personally." This from a little well-dressed man I'd never seen before. "But I know tired, friend, and you look it. What do you say I fix you up with a little pick-me-up?" I thought he was going to buy me a drink, but he pulled a bottle from his coat pocket.

Terkle leaned toward the little man and said, "This here is my place of business. The only joy juice served in here is served by me."

"Friend, this ain't liquor. Why, it's the farthest thing from it. This here is Indiana Dan's Most Potent Elixir, guaranteed to set your clock, to clean your cogs and to straighten your crookeds. Why, I'll have you know that the governor of Kansas swears by this fabulous liquid, which is for either external or internal use, depending on the nature of the problem and the desired effect."

We all just kinda looked at him. I was of a mind to try some of the stuff, but Wide grabbed the little fella by the front of his waistcoat and said, "What's your name?" Wide was mean like that, for no reason and at any time. Terk once conjectured that Wide was unable to piss. He said

8

he'd seen Wide in the bar for five and six hours straight, drinking beer after shot after beer and never once walking outside to even things out.

"Greenfeld," the man said.

Wide looked at Terkle and frowned, then offered his frown to me and the other men in turn. Then, to the little man, "What kinda damn name is that?" and he gave him a little shake which I know the little man was sorry about immediately because a playing card shook loose from somewhere and fluttered to the floor and all eyes fell to it.

Taharry said, "Tacheater."

So, everybody grabbed Greenfold and managed to get a lick in, exceptin' me. I took the opportunity to sneak a taste of the bottle of his elixir that had been left unattended on the bar. The stuff made me gag something awful and then I was bent over trying to throw up and making a devilish noise that caused the men to leave off beatin' poor Greenbelt and so allowing him to scamper across the floor and out.

I take credit now for having saved the little man's life, but at the time it didn't sit well with the men in the bar, who were, if not mad, at least disappointed that the drink had not caused me to suffer a horrible and amusing death that they could have claimed later to have witnessed. Instead, I didn't even throw up. To show their displeasure they abandoned any interest in the misdeeds done to my property and person. Except for Terkle, who reminded me of my debt.

Then Wide came back and picked up the arrow again. "What you need is a tracker."

Without looking up from the new hand of cards being dealt at the table, Taharry said, "Tabbuba tin tatown."

"Who's Tabubba?" I asked Terk.

"Bubba."

"Oh." I knew who Bubba was. Bubba was the black scout. Taharry was right. Bubba was the best tracker in the territory. A legend. A nigger. And perhaps for that reason, I suspect, basically agreeable. "Yeah," I said, more to myself than to those ignoring me at the bar, "Bubba can help me identify this arrow and then help me find my Sadie."

I stood there for a while trying to inhale the last fumes of my whiskey from the glass, listening to Terkle drum his fingers on the bar, watching Taharry spit all over the other filthy bums at the card table and standing close enough to consider myself beneath the stench of Wide Clyde. I had read what I could of the dime novels about the frontier, thinking it my duty as a citizen of it to make sure the truth be told, and generally the little books gave a fair account, but always failed to mention the smell. Hell, we hardly ever bathed and our stomachs were always grumbling and complaining and we wore our boots without stockings. If a vulture wouldn't attack us alive, it sure as hell wouldn't light on us dead. Out of good sense, we lived far from one another. We came together in bars and churches more or less to assure ourselves that our smells were normal and not an indication of coming death.

There had been a bathhouse in town. It had been owned by a tall, lean man who, and this was the general impression, bathed too much. Seemed to make sense to me. The man had himself three tubs and all the soap anybody could want. I guess he just smelled too nice or something because he made everybody nervous. Why, he'd come into the general store or the stagecoach office and folks would just shut up and breathe. He smelled so good in fact that he kinda quieted down everybody else's stink. He was around for about a year until Wide Clyde shot him dead. Wide claimed he caught the skinny man peeking through a curtain when he rose up to wash his fanny. That's how Wide reported it, too. He said, "I pushed on the sides of the tub and rose my fanny out of the water so I could give it a few dry swipes with my rag and there he was, peeking from behind that yellow blanket hanging in the doorway. He'd seen my body parts, so I shot him." They boarded up the store front and I don't know what became of the tubs, but I don't think Wide Clyde McBride got one.

I walked outside and grabbed my horse and led him alongside the boards past the general store and the stagecoach office and round past a line of troughs and into the livery. It was pretty dark, but I could see, because there was a big moon and the barn doors were wide open, I suppose to let the animals have a little air. It was a hot night and sticky and the livery smelled something fierce. At least the heat had slowed the beasts down to where they weren't stirring up the air more than necessary. I loosened my horse's girth and let the saddle fall to the ground. There weren't no one around, so I just tied him to a post and kicked some hay in front of him. He looked at me with what I thought was contempt, like he was thinking why I had to ride him so hard that day and so I said to him, "Shut up and eat."

I loosened my britches and laid down on a haystack and closed my eyes.

2

THE MORNING CAME WITH some harsh light through the open doors and the clanging and puffing of the blacksmith's labor. I looked at the man and I knew he couldn't have been there for but a few minutes, but he was a-sweatin' and a-pantin' like nobody's business and he was giving me unfriendly glances. He saw that I was awake and sitting up and so he put down his hammer and let go his bellows and walked toward me, wiping his hands on his apron.

"You sleep here all night?" he asked me.

"No," I told him.

"How long then?"

"Couple hours."

"You owe me two bits."

"For what?"

"Lodging," he said and spat on the ground. "And stablin' your horse. That is your horse."

"Yeah, he's mine."

"Two bits."

"Can we work something out?" I did up my trousers and tried to hold back my urge to piss right there in front of him.

"Sure. You pay me two bits and I won't take my hammer and beat you silly."

"I don't have any money."

"I'll keep your saddle then until you get my money," he said. "Though I can't say it's even worth two bits itself."

"Renegades attacked my spread and killed my stock and run off with my woman and even murdered my dog." I looked at his expressionless face. "Did you hear me? I said they murdered my dog."

A single tear emerged from the corner of his left eye and slid down his cheek. He turned and went back to his work, whistling a sad melody. I was unsure of my standing with him, but as he was ignoring me, I took the opportunity to piss in the corner of a stall. Then I collected my saddle and horse and started out. I stopped at the open doors and asked,

"Where can I find Bubba?"

He answered without looking up. "Was here. Gone now."

"Where to?"

"Don't keep track of niggers."

There was a boy standing at the doors. He was about twelve or so and he'd been there the while, listening. He looked dumb and I knew he didn't belong to the blacksmith 'cause of the way the man shook his iron at him. The boy watched me turn out and down alongside the livery, then he followed. I was at a trough, my horse drinking while I splashed water on my face, when I looked up and noticed him again. His hair was bright yellow with the sun behind him and I had a mind to rub his head for luck.

"What you want, boy?" I asked.

14

"I heard you say what happened to your wife," he said, looking down at his shoes.

"Yeah?"

"Was they white men?"

"Don't know for certain. They looked white, but that don't mean a hill of beans if they wasn't." I studied the expression on his face. "You know Bubba?"

The boy nodded.

"Know where he is?"

"No." He looked at the sky. "A bunch of white men killed my parents." He turned to me with his eyes all teared up. "I thought we was supposed to worry 'bout Injuns."

"Tough luck, boy."

"You going after 'em?" he asked, stepping closer.

"What business is it of yourn?"

"Why else would you need a tracker? Take me with you. I'll help you kill 'em."

"Somebody been slipping whiskey in your mama's teat? Get on away from around me, boy."

"Please, take me with you." And then he was down on his knees. "Please," he said again. "I won't get in the way. I can cook and load rifles and pistols and take care of horses."

"Go on, boy."

He walked on his knees to me, his hands together, still begging. He dropped to all fours and tried to kiss my boots, but I jumped away.

"Hey, what you doin' there? Stop it."

"Please," he said to the ground.

"No," I said.

Then he started growlin', honest to God, growlin' like a hound and he moved to me quicker than a snake and the next thing I knew he was biting my leg. I screamed and kicked him loose and damn if he didn't make another dash for me, his crooked little teeth flashing between barks. He chased me and I climbed up onto a stack of barrels for safety.

"Okay, okay," I said.

"You'll take me with you?"

"Yeah, just call yourself off."

He stood up on two feet like he'd been doin' it all his life and knocked the dust from the knees of his britches. I climbed down and watched him closely. I walked to my horse and plopped the saddle on his back, reached underneath and cinched him up.

"Where to first?" the boy asked.

"You got a name?"

"Jake." He smiled eagerly. "Where to first?"

"The saloon."

And damn if he didn't follow me closer than a noon shadow to the tavern. I tied my horse at the corner of the building and stopped Jake at the door. "They won't let you inside, so wait here," I told him. I left him standing there outside the swinging doors like the dummy he was.

In the saloon I walked to the bar and nodded a howdy to Terkle, who just grumbled back at me.

"How's about a shot on the house, Terk."

"How's about you going out there and eating some horse pucky."

"Now is that any way to be?" I glanced at the doors and couldn't see the boy's legs. I thought maybe he'd gotten tired and wandered off. That was the problem with the day's youth, no stick-to-itness. I hadn't been gone as long as a horse fart and he'd already given up on me.

16

I looked at Terk again and resigned myself to the fact that I'd get nothing from him for free. So, I asked him if he knew where I could find Bubba, since the black man wasn't at the livery.

"Nope," was what he said.

I looked around the room and locked eyes with the only other person there, Weird Wally the wheelwright. Our three eyes held fast for a second, then I walked toward him and he looked back down at his glass. His empty socket was none too pleasant to actually see close up, but it was a curious thing and something that a man would want to say that he had seen.

"Morning, Wally," I said.

"Yep," he said.

"Buy me a drink?" I asked him and tossed a glance back at Terkle.

"Nope."

"You know where I can find Bubba, the black scout?"

"Yep."

"Where? Is he in town?"

"Nope."

"Well, where is he, Wally?"

Wally didn't say anything, just scratched an itch in the upper ridge of his empty socket.

"You gonna make me guess?"

"Yep."

I sat down in the chair next to him, put my elbow on the table and rested my head in my hand. I looked at his filthy clothes and his matted beard. I hated him. "What if'n I threaten to shoot you? Will you tell me then?"

"Nope."

"Is he south of town?"

"Nope."

"North of town?"

"Yep."

"At the Simpson spread?"

"Nope."

I proceeded to name every ranch I knew, north, south, east and west of town, until I hit on the Tucker place and he finally took a breath, sighed and said—

"Yep."

I was fit to be tied and madder than a teaser when I at last got myself away from him. I moved toward the back door and I heard Terkle call out,

"Wally, another drink?"

"Yep."

I slipped out the door into the alley and walked quietly to the street. My horse was right where I'd left him. I could see his rump. I'd just jump on him and ride away out of town, leaving the stupid little tow-headed retard behind. But when I got to my pony the boy was sitting in the saddle just as pretty as a picture.

"Get down offa there," I told him.

"You was tryin' to leave without me." He stared at me and held fast to the horn with both hands.

"Show me some quarter, boy. I ain't no nursemaid. I don't know how to handle no young'un. How old are you? Eleven? Twelve?"

"Fifteen and I can take care of myself."

"Get down off my horse."

"Nope."

"Now, don't you start that stuff with yeps and nopes. Dang fool says only that and you're supposed have some kinda conversation with the filthy scumwagon. Yep and

18

nope, yep and nope. Who can get a rabbit's turd o' sense out of a man who says two confounded words? And you know he knows more. Got to." I guess I got carried away a little bit because the boy was staring at me like I had a horse's prick hanging out of my britches. Looking back now, I know it was my chance to lose him by making him think I was crazy, but it slipped past me at the time.

So, with the boy riding behind me in the saddle, I steered my horse north out of town. My stomach was beginning to complain, but it was sadly the case that neglect was all I'd be able to offer it for some time. I felt the weight of the boy's head on my back and soon heard his snoring. If he was fifteen, I was a seven-foot-tall Indian. I had a mind to let him slide from the saddle and to gallop away, but I found myself unable to do it. I mean, the little varmint might have starved to death out in the wilderness, though I wasn't exactly offering him any sustenance. Maybe the boy was good at finding food, in which case he'd come in handy. Maybe he knew where all the water holes were in the territory. Maybe he knew where there was buried treasure.

The Tucker place was fifteen miles out of town and it was mid-afternoon when I could finally see the house there on the valley floor. It was a fine place, green, gently rolling, and twisting through it was the sweetest river you'd ever put sight to. It was the kind of place that almost made you understand why the Injuns was so mad about white folks taking over.

Old man Tucker was splitting wood just outside his log house when we rode up. I tipped my hat to him and offered a friendly grin. I said, "Howdy, Mr. Tucker."

Tucker gave me a hard look, the kind of look we

westerners cultivate for people who ride onto our land grinning, and he asked, "I know you?"

"We've met," I told him. "Name's Curt Marder. My spread, well, what's left of it after the heathens got through and done with it, is southwest of here."

"You owe me money?"

"No, sir," I answered quickly. I can't say I rightly know if I spoke the truth. This obsession with money was a general and apparently necessary condition, and it was more than just a little sad to observe.

"Then what's your business here?" he asked.

I climbed down from my horse, forgetting the boy behind me, who was still asleep, surprisingly, and more so for him than for me as he fell out of the saddle and hit the ground with a violent thud before I was good and down. The fall woke him and saved Tucker asking if he was alive.

"I'm trying to find Bubba," I said.

"Bubba who?"

"I don't know his last name. Hell, he's a nigger and he probably ain't got no last name. How many Bubbas you know, anyhow?"

"I know one."

"Well, he's the one I'm looking for," I said.

"Why? You family?"

I narrowed my eyes to slits and leaned the man's way, my right hand hovering out from my gun side, my fingers spreading and twitching.

"I was just funnin' you," Tucker laughed. "Havin' a little joke, is all. What do you want with ol' Bubba?"

"I want to hire him."

"He's already working for me. Mending fence. I got a lot of fence."

"I need a tracker," I said.

Jake, who was fully awake now, stood beside me and said, "We need us a tracker."

"You do now, do you?" Tucker looked at the boy closely, then me less so. "Why?"

"Renegades killed my ma and pa," Jake said.

"Killed my dog," I added.

Tucker looked at me like I had belched out the words, then back at Jake. "I'm sorry, boy. That's an awful thing, a real awful thing."

"They rode off with my woman," I added, but it was too late; the damn child had upstaged me. I thought to mention that my parents too were dead, but instead I let it go.

"And we're going to track 'em down and kill 'em," Jake said through uneven breathing.

"Brave lad," Tucker said to the little ham. "Bubba's out on the fence north of here. Ride up river. You'll come to him."

A woman appeared at the open door of the cabin. She had dark skin and two thick braids of black hair falling from her head. She looked at us with big eyes, a deer's eyes, dark and fierce, and then to Tucker. She said something I couldn't make out and Tucker said,

"Not now. Go on back in the house."

"Your woman?" I asked.

"Yep. A good woman. Won't speak English for nothing, though. I've kinda made learning the letters a game. She's taken to that."

"She's pretty," I told him.

"She's strong," he said. "Pretty don't mean squat out here. Hell, I ain't pretty."

21

"Well, I guess we'll ride on and find Bubba."

"And you sure as hell ain't pretty. And Bubba ain't pretty. The closest thing to pretty round here is that little one with you."

I backed away, pulling my horse with me.

3

I CAN'T SAY THAT I really enjoyed talking to Tucker. He struck me as kind of a snooty fella who probably thought he was better than most folks. I can't abide by that sort of behavior. I mean, what if everybody walked around thinking that way? I mean, what kind of sense would that make?

"I don't think he liked you," Jake said, behind me in the saddle once again.

"Well, now, he don't rightly know me, does he?"

"Guess not."

"And what does he know? He's married to that heathen woman and she's got him so magick-ed up that he don't even know she's pretty. Married to a squaw."

"Sure is a fine place," the boy said.

I looked at the river and the valley and the gentle green hillside we were climbing and groaned an agreement. "If you got fine land like this, you're rich. Why, you don't even have to work, just turn the stock loose and watch 'em get big and fat. Hell, other people'd even pay you to let their cattle munch your pastures. Timin', that's the secret. Gettin' to the land before everybody else. That's what this country's all about."

"You ever met Bubba?" Jake asked.

"No."

"How will we know him?"

"He's a nigger, boy."

"Oh."

I looked around again and breathed in the thin air. "You're right though, boy. This sure is a pretty place."

Bubba was mending fence about a half a mile upriver. He saw us coming, I know, but he kept on working like we didn't matter none. Me and Jake dismounted and walked to him.

"Bubba?"

The black man peeled off his gloves and studied my face. "I know you?"

"Not yet. Curt Marder."

"What's your business?" he asked. He tossed a glance at the boy beside me.

"How do you know this ain't a social call."

"Your color and mine."

"Christ, man, it's 1871, ain't you people ever gonna forget about that slavery stuff?"

"What do you want?"

I turned to Jake. "Boy, go get that arrow outa my saddle bag." I looked to Bubba. "I want you to look at somethin' for me."

Jake came back with the thing and I gestured for him to hand it over to Bubba. Bubba looked at it and said, "It's an arrow."

"Hell, I know that. What else?"

"Been shot into something." He hardly looked at the damn thing.

"It was used to kill my dog."

24

"It could do that."

"What tribe, Bubba. Tell me what tribe uses arrows like that."

He handed the arrow back to me and stuffed his gloves into his hip pocket. "No tribe," he said. "Indians take pride in their arrows. Look at that sloppy tying job. Those are chicken feathers, not hawk or eagle. That there's the work of a white man. A white man named Donald Gerlach."

"How can you tell all that?"

"Man signed the shaft. Work may be sloppy, but your boy was proud of it."

"He—they took my woman," I told him.

"I'm sorry. That's a bad thing." He walked over to his mule and took a drink from his canteen. "Is that all you needed?"

"I want you to help me find her."

The black man laughed. Then he stopped laughing and looked at me. He laughed again.

"I need your help, man. Word is, you're the best tracker around." I was begging a nigger and I felt my belly turning over and I didn't like it.

"Let me get this straight. You want me to ride all over creation trackin' a bunch of violent white men."

"Yep."

"Marder, this is the United-goddamn-States of America. What happens when we find them? I shoot somebody so I come back here and get hanged. I don't think so."

"I'll pay you."

He looked at me really hard this time, at my clothes and boots and even over at my horse. "What you gonna pay me with, chief? You don't look flush."

Well, dang if people in these parts weren't obsessed with

money and figuring who had it and who didn't. He was right; I couldn't pay. "I'll give you my homestead. It's a full fifty-two acres. I'll give you all of it."

"All of it?"

"I'll give you six acres."

Bubba smiled a smile I didn't like. I looked over at Jake and nodded for him to speak. He cleared his throat and squeaked out with,

"They killed my ma and pa. I watched them. I was hiding behind the trough in the pigpen and they shot 'em, both of 'em." Tears were flowing now, and I tried to see if they were having any effect on the black man. I couldn't tell. "Please, help us," the boy said.

Bubba looked at me and said, "Fifty acres."

I was into it now, but it was a matter of honor, getting my Sadie back from those filthy heathen renegades. "C'mon, man," I said.

"Split it down the middle, I choose the line." He stared hard into my eyes and I knew I had to agree to his terms. That was a new experience for me, having a nigger stare right into my eyes. It kind of unnerved me, like he was working some kind of voodoo magic on me.

"Down the middle, you choose the line."

He looked at me, then spit on the ground, then put his hand out for me to shake. I stared at his hand, and he said, "Your word will do until we get it all written down."

Things were starting to cloud up considerable as far I was concerned—standing out on the range making land deals with a nigger, watching my estate suffer, to my thinking, coerced division. I had a mind to shoot Bubba for attempting to violate me, and I could now appreciate why Wide Clyde had plugged the lanky bath man.

"You know how to write, do you?" I said.

"I do. And we write it all down so there's no misunderstandin', so everything'll be proper."

I looked at Jake beside me. "What about the boy? He ain't mine. What you want him to pay you?"

"I ain't workin' for him. He didn't say he'd pay me."

"But you're helpin' him just the same as you're helpin' me. These vermin killed his mama and daddy just as sure as they run off with my Sadie. What's he gonna pay you?"

Bubba looked at the boy and kinda smiled at him. "I'm doin' him a favor."

I didn't let on how unfair I thought all of it was. I just nodded and looked at the sky, not that the sky had given me much in the way of understanding in my life, but I didn't have nowhere else to look.

"We'll need supplies," Bubba said, walking back to his mule and stuffing his gloves into a saddle bag. "Grub, ammo, gunpowder, coffee."

I said okay and then added that I was a little short on cash and he wanted to know how short and I said, "Well, it's like this—"

And he cut me off with a raised hand, grumbled and muttered, "I'm keepin' a tab and you're paying me back."

This western setup I felt was in the long run destined to be self-defeating. Me and Bubba and this boy tearing across the territory in search of my woman, facing death at the hands of Injun impersonators. But I was bound to do it. That was the code, our code, the code of the frontier.

"You go to town and get the supplies. Put it on my tab. I'll be in the barn at Tucker's place." He got on his mule.

"Come on, boy," I said and walked to my horse.

"I'll wait here," Jake said.

I looked at him and then at Bubba.

"That's fine," Bubba said.

So, with the sun halfway between midday and setting, I was riding back to the pissant little town. My fanny and thighs were sore from all the time on the leather, and I had to tilt my hat forward against the sun, which was hurting my eyes. The rhythmic clip-clopping of my horse's hooves on the dry trail must have lulled me into some kind of state, because I saw my Sadie plain as anything with the vermin who stole her. She was wearing the blue dress, her only dress, but she was smiling, smiling at me and I didn't understand and I wanted to ask why, but she weren't real, just a thing in my head. I snapped awake as my horse tripped a bit on a stone.

It was night when I got to town, and I found the general store locked and dark. I didn't cotton to the idea of another night in the livery, especially not to the notion of waking to that strange blacksmith, so I decided I'd sleep outside of town in my bedroll. But I stopped off at the saloon to see if my situation could be advertised as dire enough to squeeze a sympathy drink out of Terkle.

The town was more crowded than the previous night. Gloria, the lone saloon girl, was standing next to the piano whining a sad song while the piano man pounded out something different on the keys. There were a couple of poker games going on, and at one table sat Wide Clyde McBride and Taharry, who waved hello.

I nodded a greeting to Terkle, but he just shook his head, turned away and moved toward the far end of the bar. There would be no free drinks from him, so I went and sat at the table with Wide and Taharry and another real skinny fellow I didn't know. Wide was shuffling and cuttin a deck of cards with blue backs.

"Tahowdy."

"Evenin', Taharry," I said. "Wide." I nodded to the stranger.

"Find the heathens yet?" Wide asked without looking up from the cards.

"No, but I found Bubba. He's gonna track 'em for me."

"Tahe'll tafind ta'em."

"How come you ain't drinking?" Wide asked.

"No money."

Wide nodded knowingly.

"Long, hard, dusty trail," I said.

"Maybe you can win you some money and buy yourself a drink," Wide said.

"Can't win money if you ain't got none to start with," I told him.

"You got land, don't you?"

"Yeah."

"How much land you got, Marder?" Wide asked.

"Fifty-two acres."

Wide smiled and let loose a little whistle. "That's a nice chunk of land. Fifty-two acres? How about that? It was meant to be, Marder. Fifty-two acres, fifty-two cards in a deck. See. An omen. This is probably your lucky night."

"Well, I was gonna use part of that land to pay Bubba."

Wide stopped fussing with the cards and looked at me. "Pay him with land? Is that legal, for a nigger to own land?" When I said nothing, he looked to Taharry.

"Taprobably tanot."

"I don't know," Wide said, shaking his big head. "You might want to check on that." He drained his glass of the last swallow of whiskey and slammed it on the table as a signal to Terk that he wanted more. "Tell you what, Marder. I'll front you a little money to get you started in the game."

I licked my lips as I watched Terk come over and pour more whiskey into Wide's glass.

"Bring Marder a drink," Wide said. "On me." He looked at my eyes. "You're playin', right?"

"I'm in," I said.

He pushed a little pile of money across the table to me.

While Wide shuffled the cards, Terk came back with a glass for me, which he dropped loudly down on the table and then filled with whiskey. I picked up the drink and took a sip. It burned my parched lips and then my throat. Wide pushed the deck in front of me for cutting and said —

"Cut 'em the way you like 'em."

I cut the cards.

Wide said, "Marder, this here is Skinny Finney." He pointed to the lanky stranger.

Finney nodded his long horse's head at me and smiled a toothy grin.

I felt the fingers of luck tickling at my belly. This was my night, I just knew it. Lady Luck was sitting in my lap. I gave the money in front of me a touch, and it felt hotter than a horse fart. I watched the cards slip from Wide's chubby fingers, and I watched close to be sure he wasn't dealing from the bottom. Personally, I always wait until all my cards have been dealt before I pick them up, unlike some fellas who pick them up one at a time as they land. I like the full, sudden effect, especially if there are face cards in the hand. So, I picked them up and fanned them out, and there it was, Lady Luck sitting full on my face, three sixes and two jacks. I cleared my throat and took a sip of whiskey and gave sidelong glances to the other men. I put my cards face down in front of me.

The betting started modestly and real friendly-like, so I got comfortable with the warm feeling the whiskey was putting in my belly. Wide asked about cards. Taharry took two and Skinny Finney took three. I stood pat and tried not to smile while Wide took three. I tossed another buck into the pot, which was seen, then raised two more by Wide. Taharry folded. I saw Wide's bet, then Finney did the same and called. I won the hand. My money was doubled and I felt giddy. I pushed Wide's initial loan back to him and thanked him proper-like.

The playing went like that, all these good cards coming my way and my little pile of money growing into a big pile of money. Wide kept on smiling the while and laughing here and there and slapping my shoulder. I was laughing too and buying my own drinks.

Terk came over to the table at one point and reminded me of the three dollars I owed him, but Wide just pushed him away, saying, "Can't you see the man's busy playin' cards?" Wide leaned toward me and said, "This is just killin' him, ain't it? Seein' you with all that money."

I laughed with him.

Taharry laughed, too: "Taha, taha, taha."

Things changed, though. I was dealt a hand that was less pretty. I held a pair of eights and nothing else. I took three and got a pair of jacks in the trade. I felt real fine once again, sitting there lookin' at those boys in my hand. The betting took a more serious tone and Finney folded, and shortly thereafter Taharry said, "Tai'm taout."

It was just Wide and me left, and my pile of cash was

gettin' slight. He reached into his pocket and dumped a hundred dollars into the pot.

I laughed. "I don't have that kind of money. You know I don't have that kind of money."

"So, you're out then?" Wide smiled big.

I looked at all that money in the pot and at those pretty boys in my hand. Two pair. I looked at Wide's face. He couldn't beat two pair. I tried to catch the reflection of his cards in his fat eyes. He was bluffing and I knew it. "Will you take my marker?" I asked.

The way he laughed, you would have thought I'd asked him to marry me. "I don't know, Marder," he said. "I don't see that your marker's gonna be worth very much. I mean, you havin' outstanding debt as it is. You know, owing Terk money and all."

"I've got land." It just came out.

Wide hummed a consideration. "Land. Yes, that might do. Go ahead, write it down. Throw your spread into the pot. I'll let you do that. Wait, I'll write it and you sign it."

He wrote it down and passed the paper to me:

Curt Marder owes Clyde McBride 52 ackers of land, namely his homsted, namely all the land he poseses.

I signed it and put it in the middle of the table. I called.

Wide laid down his cards. I thought I was going to bite off my tongue, because there they were, four big, fat aces. Wide laughed and threw his head back on his thick neck like he was some kind of devil.

"Tawow."

I watched as the fat man raked in his winnings with his forearms. I felt hollow and sick.

"You got a deed to your place?" Wide asked.

"Burned up in the fire."

"That's no matter," he said. "I'll just wander over to the land office in the morning with this piece of paper and get one."

"One more hand," I said.

"Afraid not, boy." Wide knocked back a drink. "You're busted."

He laughed again as he got up and waddled away to the bar. Taharry and Skinny Finney followed, slapping him on the back.

I reached for the last bit of whiskey in my glass and found Terkle taking it away from me. "You get out of my establishment before I shoot you."

I left.

4

SOMEWHERE OUT IN THE deep night was a hoot owl that wouldn't shut up. I was tucked into my roll trying to warm up against the chill in the air, and that damn bird kept on whoing. Finally, I pulled my gun and split the dark with a shot. That quieted the critter—for a while. I was just about asleep, my ears still ringing from the shot, when the owl started in again, closer this time. I was sick about the poker game, and I thought of finding Wide, which wouldn't be hard, and shooting him, but I was afraid of him, a condition I had found to be a reliable deterrent to senseless and regrettable violence. Anyway, I was unsure how much damage a bullet might do, having to penetrate all that blubber. Certainly, there were organs underneath, but God only knew how far down. I was mad at myself for letting the green smell of money cloud my brain, but that aroma of cash, that perfume of winning had just been so powerful—so strong, in fact, that I'd been immune to the ever-present reek of Wide Clyde McBride.

Owl and all, I closed my eyes and imagined the coming recovery of my Sadie. I recalled how on chilly nights in the cabin her warm body under the blankets made me comfortable and how I just hated it when she left the bed in the mornings, left me alone there in the bed, to cook up breakfast. Where was she now, my Sadie? I had to get to her before she was spoiled by her devilish captors. Sleep at last came to me as I lay counting the calls of the owl.

I was fairly well rested by the time morning saw me into town. The sky was a deep blue without even a suggestion of a cloud. As I rode down the main thoroughfare I was struck by the number of men who had a gun strapped to their side but who, like me, would rather have put their head up a cow's ass than draw the damn thing.

I tied my horse outside the general store and found Jan Petersen, the big Swede who limped, helping some fella load his buckboard with sacks of feed. It was early in the morning, but Petersen had already worked up a monstrous sweat. He had huge arm muscles and a huge chest, which was bare under his apron. He made me feel puny, and to my thinking his mass made him seem the smarter. He finished loading and, with his yellow teeth showing in a smile, turned to find me. I suppose I had yellow teeth too but somehow, I guess since I didn't have to look at them, they never bothered me.

"Come to settle accounts, Marder?" he asked.

Again this regional obsession with money had raised its ugly head. I said, "I'm afraid not, Petersen. Of course, you done heard the news of my grave misfortune."

Petersen looked at me for a second, then said, "Oh, yeah. I was awfully sorry to hear about your dog. Just what is this territory coming to? It's the whole country."

"That's what I say. I had to stand witness to it all. I just found Bubba and he done agreed to help me track down the dirty no-good-fers."

He nodded, turned and led the way into the store. I followed him, resisting the urge to imitate his limp. It was a hard hop to leave alone and more than a handful of men had been beaten senseless by the Swede's big arms after he caught them walking like him.

Inside, he said, "Bubba's a good tracker."

"That's what I hear."

"Oh, he's a good one, all right. Yeah, you got yourself one hell of a tracker. He's a good man too. It's a shame he's a nigger. He's polite. Well, hell, he's downright respectful. Course, he's a black man. You know he saved my life once? I ain't ashamed to admit it. A cougar had me cold. I didn't have nowhere to run." Petersen slid in behind the counter and let up on his story as the bell on the front door jingled.

Pickle Cheeseboro, the preacher, was inside with us. He was dressed all in black except for his blood-red vest, a small man made smaller by the oversized black hat he wore, and his face was pocked horribly. "Mornin', Jan," Cheeseboro said. He looked to me and nodded.

"Preacher," I said, though I didn't know the man well, especially not in his professional capacity.

Petersen perked up at the sudden doubling of his audience and began again with vigor. "I was just tellin' Marder here about how Bubba the black scout saved my life." He leaned against the counter. "You see, I was out huntin' in Sidewinder Canyon, lookin' for an elk to get me through winter, from this herd that the stagecoach driver, Fuzzy Cussworth, had told me he'd seen. Well, I was on the trail of a big one. I was off my horse, scrabblin' over the rocks, when I saw the lion. That was when I slipped and dropped my gun, and I swear the beast had me cornered good. I couldn't get to my rifle, and I was about to make my peace with the Almighty"—he looked to the preacher for acknowledgment—"when out of nowhere pops that nigger."

"He was sent by God, brother," Pickle Cheeseboro said.

"Must have been," Petersen said, "because up he popped from behind a boulder and drew a bead on that critter faster than a stuck pig squeals and shot him, bang, right between the eyes." Petersen looked at each of us in turn, nodding. "Didn't even wait around for me to thank him."

"Where would a nigger learn manners?" the preacher said.

"That's what I said," Petersen agreed. "Can't blame him for what he is."

"Well put," said Pickle Cheesboro.

"Anyway, Marder here has done hired Bubba to help track down the filthy bastards what killed his dog. Excuse my language, preacher."

"I was sad to hear of your misfortune," Pickle Cheeseboro said to me. "And they are indeed bastards," he said to Petersen. "There is no blasphemy when the truth is spoken, brother."

I left them to talk while I collected sundries from the shelves. I grabbed sugar, flour, coffee and all the time I was feeling ill. As if it hadn't been enough to assume an attitude of supplication to a negroid individual and in so doing compromise my estate, I had also to gather these supplies and put them on the black man's tab. It was downright embarrassing, degrading even. I glanced out the window and down the street and saw Wide Clyde McBride squeezing himself out of the land office. He was smiling, so I knew

38

he'd gotten the deed to my spread. I'd have to keep this news from Bubba.

I set the goods on the counter and asked Petersen to add some jerky to the lot. He turned to take it from the sack on the shelf behind him and I smiled at Pickle Cheeseboro.

"Be sure to pray," Pickle said to me. "It takes only a few seconds and it will save your life. Both in the short run and the long." He nodded reassuringly.

"I'll be sure to do it," I said, thinking I could talk to God until I was blue in the face and that wouldn't change the way He hated me. I would have hated Him back, except that I was scared of Him. Like my daddy said, "Never hate anybody you're a-scared of; it's a waste of time."

"Just a few seconds," Pickle repeated and reached inside his black coat and gave his little red vest a tug at its bottom.

"That enough jerky?" Petersen asked.

"Yeah, I think so."

"You know, you might fare a little better with the bad boys if you took a mess of bullets along with you." Petersen gave me a little yellow smile.

"Yep. Better let me have a few boxes of shells. You would have thought Bubba would have remembered to put that on the list."

"How you payin'?" Petersen asked, his tone different.

"Put it on Bubba's tab," I said.

Petersen and Cheeseboro exchanged glances and then Petersen said, "I'll do that. Yeah, that Bubba's a good tracker. He pays real regular too. Of course, he has to, if you know what I mean." He laughed.

Pickle Cheesboro laughed too.

"You give those dog-killin' bastards what for," Petersen said.

"Yes indeed," Pickle said. "Remember to pray and your hills will be leveled and valleys will be raised, your crookeds will be straightened and your nights will be made like day."

"That was beautiful, preacher," Petersen said.

"A piece of the sermon I'm workin' on for this comin' Sunday. It's a little diddy on the sin of mixin', if you know what I mean."

"Oh, I know, I know," said Petersen.

"You got a sack I can put this stuff in?" I asked.

5

WITH THE GOODS IN my saddle bags I set out on the trail
back to the Tucker place. The long ride ahead was not attractive, but the longer I tarried in town, the more distance
I'd put between me and my Sadie. As the miles slipped by,
I thought about how often lately I was sleeping in my
clothes. And I considered again Wide Clyde sucking me
into that poker game. If he wasn't a cheat, then he missed
being one by the width of a baby's hair. I saw a little smoke
rising from the hills to the east, and much of the rest of
my ride was consumed with long head-turnings and neck-
stretchings for any unannounced riders. If I had been with
a posse, I'd have been galloping along. For some reason,
horses don't get tired in a bunch. I reckon they find some
comfort in looking over and finding a sweaty wither or
haunch. Misery loves company.

The waning day had cooled considerable by the time I
reached Tucker's place. Bubba's mule was tied up by the
hand pump in the front of the house, but there weren't nobody in sight. I dismounted and walked to the door, listening for voices. I didn't want to happen on to Tucker in the
middle of his privates and get him mad at me. At the door

I heard Tucker talking and then Bubba talking, so I knocked.

Jake opened the door and stepped aside to let me in.

"You all havin' a howdy do in here?" I asked.

Tucker looked at me in the middle of the awkward silence and then said, "Sit down, Martin. We were just talkin'. Anything worth seeing in town?"

"It ain't burned to the ground yet," I said. I sat down at the table with them and looked over at the squaw who was tending a pot on the stove. She put another piece of wood into the fire and gave me a sidelong glance.

"I was tellin' Bubba and the young'un about this Mormon elder I met in Salt Lake who had two hundred fifty wives," Tucker said.

"No such thing," I said.

"Two hundred fifty, sure as pigs eat snakes." He reached behind him and slapped his wife on her ample rump and said, "You remember that man with all them wives."

She ignored him.

"I asked him how come he came to have so many and he said he married one, liked her, married her sister, liked her, married her mother, her cousin and that's how it got started. I asked him how come he didn't marry none of her brothers and uncles. That's when he left off talkin' to me. Them Mormons can be sensitive about their families and they're violent too, so we rode outa them parts pronto."

I looked at Bubba. He was just listening while he sharpened his knife with a round stone.

"Did you see all them wives?" I asked.

"I didn't count 'em, but there was sure enough a houseful." He put his elbows on the table and leaned forward.

"And I got the distinct impression that his favorite was this little young thing, couldn't have been more than eleven."

"You're makin' this up."

Bubba left off sharpening and looked at me and then at Tucker.

"Are you callin' me a liar?" Tucker asked. He was smiling easy, but I was troubled by his smile just the same.

"Well, no, it's that what you're sayin' is kinda hard to believe, you know? Two hundred fifty is more than most herds of cattle."

"So?"

"One bull ain't enough for a herd that size," I said. "You got cattle; you know that."

"Ain't enough for what?"

"You know."

Tucker looked at Bubba all confused-like and Bubba shrugged.

"You know what I'm talkin' about," I said to the black man. "Tell him."

Bubba shrugged once more and continued work on his blade.

"All I'm sayin' is, that sounds like an awful lot."

Tucker just smiled at me.

"But I've heard Salt Lake is a different kind of place," I said. "Never been there myself, but I heard."

Tucker looked back at his wife. "Them beans about done?"

She said something in Indian and he seemed satisfied. He looked at Jake. "How old are you?"

"Sixteen," Jake said and looked at me.

"You're little," Tucker said. "Nothin' to be ashamed of.

I was little for a big part of my life. In fact, I was little until I got big."

Jake nodded.

"This country'll make you big," Tucker said to the boy.

"Or kill you," Bubba said.

"Amen to that," Tucker said.

The smell of the beans and pork was fat in the room and it made me hungry, made my stomach rumble, and I wanted to talk.

"I love the west," I said and they all turned to me. "The west is far as I can see when I'm facin' that way." I was feelin' poetic and they was listenin'. "That's the way it's always been, the way it is and the way it's gone be. Why, a white man can come out here with nothing and die with everything."

"So, you love the west," Tucker said.

"Sure do."

"Then it's a stupid love you got."

"How you figure?" I asked.

" 'Cause the west don't love you back, son," Tucker said. "You're just whacking off in the sand. Sure, it feels all right, but you'll end up with nothing to show for it and just having to do it again. Plus, it ties up a perfectly good hand that you might be using for somethin' else."

I couldn't think of nothing to say to him. Luckily, the squaw came to the table with a stack of wooden bowls and started to dish up the beans.

We ate without talkin' for a while. The woman sat with us but never looked up from her bowl. The beans were tasty and full of salt, the way I liked.

"Slow down," Tucker said to Jake. "Plenty of time, plenty of grub."

Jake grinned and ate on.

"It's a shame about what some folks will do to other folks," Tucker said. "My best friend and his wife were bushwhacked by men who wanted the water on his land. Everybody knew who did the killin', but didn't nothing happen to 'em. Not a dag-blamed thing." He shoveled a big spoonful of beans into his mouth. "Fools ride around out here lookin' for justice."

"Out here we have to make our own," I said.

Tucker smiled at Jake and pointed to me.

I looked at Bubba. "Where do you reckon we should start?"

"Start where you saw 'em," he said.

"Makes sense." I scraped the last of the beans from my bowl.

Night came on like ink. There was no moon. I was standing out by the corral. Bubba and the boy had already bedded down in the barn, having said their farewells to Tucker and his wife because we were planning to leave early. I listened to the few horses in the pen snort and step, and I imagined that Mormon with all them wives. With that many, how would he know who was who, and who was or wasn't really one of his or one of some other man just looking for a free meal? He musta had a lot of money. I met a Mormon once and I didn't understand a word he said to me. I think he was rich, too.

In the barn, the boy and the black man were snoring away in a couple of empty stalls. The ladder up to the loft was just inside the door, so I decided to go up there for the fresh hay. I put my foot on the first rung and it broke, sending a loud snap through the silence. The momentary pause in their breathing let me know they were awake, but they didn't say nothing, so I climbed on up. I found a soft place and, chill in the air or not, shed my britches to let my body breathe. The hay was a little scratchy on my legs, but the air felt good and soon I was asleep.

6

THE BLACKENED REMAINS OF MY house and barn were still smoldering. There weren't no glowing embers to see, but smoke twisted from many points like wispy devils, and the spent lumber hissed while I relieved myself on it. The smell was strong and I could feel the heat. As I did up my pants, I watched Bubba kick through the rubble, Jake behind him at every turn. The black man would upset a timber and look under it, and the boy would hover over the same spot, darting from one side of the man to the other trying to see the observed thing. I went and stood by the chimney, the only dag-blasted thing left standing, and gazed at the hill what from I had witnessed the foul doings. I looked at the mess at my feet. There were pieces of clothes and spoons and parts of furniture that somehow managed to escape being burned at all. I spied a couple of five-cent coins and knelt to get them, found them hot to the touch. I raised my eyes up to the noon sun.

Bubba was in the yard between the house and the barn when I joined him. He spoke to me without pausing in his study of the ground. "You know how to use a gun, Marder?" he asked.

" 'Course I know how to use a gun."

"Any good?"

"I ain't no trick shot or nothing, but I hit what I aim at, mostly."

"You wouldn't never point no gun at me," he said. "I'm just askin'."

"Not unless you was trying to rob, kill, or violate me dishonorable-like." I regarded the house and the barn once again. "All this rummagin' around tell you anything yet? I mean, ain't they gettin' way ahead of us?"

"Prob'bly."

Bubba eyed something and walked toward it. He dropped to a knee and picked up a clump of dirt. Jake was right beside him, kneeling as well.

"What is it?" I asked.

"Marder, you got any red clay on your land?"

I considered the question and said that I didn't.

"Well, then." He paused. "You been around any lately?" He squinted up at me, the sun in his face.

I shook my head. "Not that I know of."

"Well, this here is red clay." He looked at the hills to the west. "If'n you didn't bring it here, maybe they brought it here. There are a couple of canyons up there with red clay. 'Course, there are a lot of places with red clay."

"What are you sayin'?"

"Ain't sayin' nothing." He pointed at the hills. "Clay says it."

"So, what now?" I asked.

"We follow the trail."

"What trail?" I looked all around. "I don't see no dagnabit trail. All I see is my poor hound that the buzzards done strewn every which way and my burnt up abode and you squattin' there holdin' what for all I know is a red horse turd."

He stood and calmly walked to his mule, put a foot in the stirrup and hoisted himself into the saddle. "Which way did you see 'em ride away?" he asked.

I pointed west.

Bubba bit off a plug of chew, got it wet, then spat juice on the ground near my feet. "That's the trail then." He looked at me and then at Jake. "Come on, boy, you can ride on with me for a while."

Jake reached up and grabbed Bubba's offered arm and fell into the saddle behind him.

I mounted and followed.

"How did you come to be a tracker?" I asked. It was afternoon now, and our pace had slowed just a little. I was riding even with Bubba and the boy.

"How's a man become anything?"

"What kinda fool answer is that?"

He didn't say anything.

Then Jake asked him, "How did you come to be one, Bubba?"

"People was always trackin' me and they was always catchin' me, too. So I just started to watchin' 'em. Soon, they was catchin' me 'cause I was too busy watchin' 'em to keep runnin'." He turned halfway in the saddle and observed Jake. "You comfortable back there?"

The boy adjusted himself in the saddle. "Yeah, I'm doin' awright."

"Not that there's much to do if'n you ain't," Bubba said.

Jake laughed.

We rode on a piece and I got to looking at his mule,

a kinda brownish-red affair, calf-kneed and fat-rumped. "That mule of yourn got a name?" I asked.

"Yep."

"Well?"

"Well, what?"

"Well, what's his name?"

"I ain't tellin' you," he said.

"Why not?"

" 'Cause, it's secret."

"You can tell me," I said.

"Then it won't be no secret."

"Secret? Come on, what's the fool thing's name? You can tell me. I ain't gonna blab it to nobody."

"You don't need to know. You got no reason to be callin' this here mule." He spat out a stream of tobacco juice.

"Lordy Christmas." He was one exasperating negroid being. "Why for you ride a mule anyway?"

"Nobody ever wonders if a mule is stole," he said.

"Why such an ugly mule?"

"Nobody wants to steal *him*."

Talking with Bubba let me hear how nice his voice sounded, but it was a dreadful failure as conversation. So, I addressed the boy—

"Hey boy, what is your full and true Christian name?"

"Jen—Jake Stinson."

"You pay attention to ol' Bubba here and maybe you'll learn yourself the trackin' business. Good to have a trade. Out here, there's always a call for good trackers, but you gotta learn it young. Ain't that right, Bubba?"

"Right," Bubba said softly and spat juice.

"Learn it while you're a pup or be born to it, which means being a nigger or an Injun or some other breed what's got a good nose and natural animal senses. Right, Bubba?"

"Right."

Bubba leaned forward in his saddle and studied the ground, kept his mule at a slow walk.

"What you seein'?" I asked him, looking down at the ground myself.

"We got us a trail, awright. Five, maybe six horses. One of 'em's a pack animal, leastways he's being led."

"Good news. You just keep it up, keep earnin' your pay and we'll catch those bastards."

"I'll do that."

I was feeling good, sitting up straight in the saddle now, and I decided to try talking to the black man again. "Where'd you come from, boy?" Young Jake looked at me, but it was Bubba I was talking to. "I mean, you, Bubba."

Bubba turned his head slowly and took me in. He spat tobacco juice at the front feet of my horse. "I ain't no boy."

"Well, what the hell you want me to call you?"

He looked at the head of his mule and, without facing me, said, "If'n you gotta call me, you might as well use my name, which you know and I don't have to tell you."

"I'll let this uppity behavior slide, Bubba, since I done hired you and all." The short exchange put a chill over our little crew. We rode on, however, stopping now and again so the black man could dismount and study tracks, or so we could rest or sprinkle the sage with piss.

Just after the coming of dusk, we stopped for the day. I hadn't known, but Bubba had gotten an extra blanket from Tucker for the boy to use as his bedroll. Jake climbed down from the saddle and hurriedly unlashed it from the mule. There wasn't nothing tied up in it, but he treated it like something special. He rolled it out onto the ground like it was a carpet of one of them desert bastards I seen in a picture book once.

Bubba called the boy to him and said, "Gather wood for the fire and start it right here. Can you do that?"

"Sure."

"Right here." Bubba marked a spot on the ground with the heel of his boot. He reached into his vest pocket, pulled out a couple of matches and placed them in Jake's hand. "Don't waste 'em now."

"Yes, sir, I mean, no, sir."

"Don't call me sir, son," Bubba said. "Just call me by my name."

"Awright, Bubba."

"Go on and get the wood."

Bubba watched the boy walk away and I stepped to his side. "Funny little fella, ain't he," I said.

"Are you sure you didn't recognize any of the men who attacked your place?" he asked me.

"I'm sure. Why you ask?"

The black man walked to his mule and uncinched his saddle. I went to my horse, which was tied next to the mule.

"Why you ask?" I repeated.

"Just askin'. Ain't many people out here in these parts. Thought maybe one of 'em might have looked familiar."

I had the leather off my horse and on the ground. "Well, they didn't. Hell, man, I couldn't even tell if'n they was white or red."

He looked at the moon, which was not quite full, and said, "Whoever they is, we're gettin' closer to 'em."

"Great."

"I didn't say we was close, just closer," he said.

Jake came back and dumped an armful of twigs and sticks on the ground. He carefully built a platform, stacking little twigs around a bit of dry-as-dust sage, then added bigger twigs. He struck a match that flashed yellow and reminded me just how dark it had gotten, and also of Swede Petersen's teeth. The first match went out before he could get it to the sage.

"Here, let me," I said.

"Let the boy do it," Bubba said, holding the coffeepot and the saddle bags of grub. "It's his job."

I stood away and watched the boy strike the second match closer to the sage and ignite it. The flame spread from the sage to the little twigs, and he leaned larger sticks onto it, and the fire crawled to them until it was all going pretty good. He came to his feet and smiled at Bubba.

Bubba nodded. "Keep feeding it, and find some rocks to put around it."

7

THE COFFEE SMELLED GOOD brewin' there over the open fire. I grabbed the pot from off the rocks and poured myself another cup. Jake scraped up the last of his beans and shoveled them into his greedy little mouth. I was a little confused why it was that we had all gotten equal portions; I mean, one of us was a nigger and another a child. Some kind of owl called out in the night, an owl like I never heard before and I looked at Bubba. He was talking to the boy.

"My folks was slaves and I was a slave," he said. "That man what owned us in Virginia liked to beat his slaves. My pa died and I run away. I run as fast and far as I could. They say we're free now. But I don't believe it. I'll always be a runaway and they'll always want to kill me."

"Are you a nigger?" Jake asked.

"No."

"Then what are you?" I asked.

"I'm a black man," he said, but he said it to the boy and not to me.

"Nigger's just a word for black man," I said.

Bubba didn't say nothing, just kind of shook his head. The strange owl called again.

Bubba looked at me. "I ain't got nothing against you personal, Marder. You cain't help it if your god made your head without a brain. But I'm helpin' you find your woman, and if'n you want my continued assistance—"

"Are you about to threaten me, boy?" I cut him off.

He looked at me for a second, then at Jake, then back at me. And he didn't say anything, just sipped his coffee.

"Do you hate Bubba?" Jake asked me.

The question came out of the blue like eagle shit and I didn't know what to say, so I said, "No, I don't hate him."

"Why you call him a nigger?"

"Cause that's what he is."

Bubba put down his cup and bit off a plug of chew. He said to Jake, "Leave off, child. Ain't worth it."

A sound came from the night, like a stick cracking, and I straightened my back and stared out into the darkness. "You hear that?" I asked.

"Like a stick breakin'?" Bubba asked.

"Yeah," I said.

"No, didn't hear it," he said.

"There it is again," I said. And that weird owl hooted funny again. "You had to hear it."

"Yeah, I heard it, Marder," the black man admitted. "There are four Indians over in them trees."

I put my hand on my gun. "How long they been there?"

"Pretty good while now."

"Why didn't you say nothing?" I gave him a mad look.

"I did say nothing." Bubba put a hand on Jake's shoulder. "It's okay, boy."

"Are they hostile?" I wanted to know. I pulled my gun free of the leather.

"Could be. They know we ain't much to reckon with."

"What's your point?"

"I'd put that away," he said. "It's possible, Marder, that they'll take that as a sign you wanna fight."

I put the gun away.

Then the black man was to his feet and facing the very trees he said the Injuns was hiding in and he was waving for them to come on out. I thought he'd lost his negro mind, so I tried to hush him up by grabbing him. You try to help a body and he throws you to the ground. While I found my legs, the Injuns wandered into the light of the fire. I stood up straight and said—

"How."

The trading of looks got kind of frenzied there for a bit, what with the Injuns looking at each other and at Bubba and Bubba looking at each one of them, and then one of the red men mocked me—

"How," he said.

"How come?" from another one.

"How about it?" said Bubba.

And the whole passel of them were having a high ol' funny at my expense. I said, "Well, pardon the hell out of me."

Before I knew it, without even a questioning look, the black man was inviting the heathens to sit and have jerky and coffee, staples that I had bought with his hard-earned money. They did sit and made themselves right comfy, crossing their feet in front of the fire and leaning back on their elbows.

Bubba started in with introductions. "Jake, this here is Big Elk, Red Eagle, Running Deer and Happy Bear. This here is Jake."

They all nodded at Jake, and the chubby one, the one

I thought must have been Happy Bear, kinda tossed a sideways glance my way.

"That's Marder," Bubba said.

"What are you doing out here?" the tallest one, who seemed to be the leader, asked.

"We're looking for some men, Big Elk," Bubba said. "Marder here had his house burnt up and he's done hired me to help him find the vermin."

"Hmmm." Big Elk looked at me. "Helping the white man find white men. And when you find them?"

"Pondering it," Bubba said.

"Ponder long."

"They was dressed up like Indians." He looked at Jake. "Go get me that arrow from the bags."

The boy got up and walked over to where the saddles were laid by the horses.

"Dressed like our people?" Big Elk asked.

"I don't know," Bubba said. "Was Marder that seen 'em." He looked at me. "What was they wearin', Marder?"

"You know, Injun clothes."

"Were they dressed like Big Elk and Happy Bear here?" he asked.

"Well, not exactly." I looked at the buckskin britches of the red men. "They had on regular britches and was wearin' feathers around their heads."

"What kind of feathers?" Happy Bear asked.

"Hell, I don't know. Bird feathers."

Jake came back and gave the arrow to Bubba, who passed it on to Big Elk. A smile worked across Big Elk's face, and as the thing got passed around among them, they got a good laugh on.

"What's so dag-blamed funny?" I wanted to know.

They started talking in heathen talk and got Bubba to laughing too.

"What in the ding-dang world is so humor-like?" I was getting mad. "Bubba?"

"They said children make better arrows in their village," Bubba said. "They said such a thing would have trouble sticking in anything."

"Tell 'em it stuck in my dog pretty good." I felt like they was making fun of white men and it made me mad. I mean, the arrow had performed its intended purpose, which was what a thing ought to do. "Tell 'em he wouldn't be no deader by one of their arrows."

They laughed harder.

"They ran off with my woman too," I said as they winded down. "They also killed the boy's ma and pa."

They stopped laughing at that point and observed young Jake. The boy had been silent the while, but he was seeming to relax with the red men in camp. Happy Bear reached over a fat hand and patted Jake's foot.

"Have you seen these men?" Bubba asked.

"No," Big Elk said.

Everybody was quiet for a while, and though I didn't want to, I felt my eyes trying to make me sleep. Running Deer left and came back with more wood. The fire glowed real bright and I was scared to let my guard down, but I was so sleepy. I could hear them talking far off.

"The white soldiers are trying to make us move again," Big Elk said. "They make a treaty with us, then break it. Make another, break it. We are weary of this. We told them we will kill them if they come. What do you think we should do, Bubba?"

"Kill 'em," Bubba said.

I wanted to say something, but I didn't.

"Always do what you say you gonna do," Bubba added.

"Why do you help this man?" Running Deer asked.

"He's gonna pay me in land," Bubba said. "Funny, ain't it. It used to be your land. Maybe I should give it back to you when I get it."

"You're darker than we are," Happy Bear said. "They won't let you keep it. Do you believe they'll let you keep it?"

"No one can own the land," Big Elk said.

"No one should own it," the black man said. "But that's the game now, Big Elk. I ask myself every morning what's a man to do. I cry about it. I get sick with it."

"How do you answer yourself, my friend?" Big Elk asked.

I couldn't really make out Bubba's response, but it sounded like "Kill 'em."

The black man and the Indians talked damn near all through the night. I'd wake up here and there and hear a red man laugh or say something or I'd hear Bubba's voice, which was deep and kind of like a song, and it'd nudge me back toward sleep.

In my head I dreamed of the territory when I first came to it. It was late summer and water was scarcer than hell. The Cahoots Rivers weren't nothing more than a bunch of puddles threaded together by a trickle. All the animals were up in the high country, and the problem was, the Injuns were up there too. It was big country and I'd wanted to see it, but it scared me something awful, like it was making threats at me all the time. Like all the settlers, I looked to taming it and making it work for me, so I could get rich. My dream had me sitting at a big table, waiting for Sadie, who was walking toward me with a dandy cooked turkey. The table was outside, beside a fine river. She put the bird down and I told her that the land was mine. I said I had a fine place and stock and that I had me a woman. She started to laugh.

8

IT WEREN'T THE LIGHT of a new morning that tugged at my sleep but the dry crunch of a boot by my head. I sat up, rubbing my face and yawning and working a tightness out of my shoulder. I observed how dark the eastern horizon was.

"Criminy jicket," I said. "It ain't even tomorrow yet." I watched as Bubba and the boy rolled up their blankets. "It ain't close to light," I said louder.

"That's right," Bubba said.

I found my legs and stepped away a couple of yards to piss on a little prickly pear. There was no sign of the Injuns. I didn't remember them leaving. Stealthy devils. I turned to notice a third horse among us. "Where'd that pony come from?" I asked.

"Happy Bear left him for me," Jake said, stepping to the animal and rubbing her snoot. "Ain't she pretty?"

"You mean, that fat Indian just up and left you an entire horse?"

Bubba was to his mule now, tossing the blanket onto its back and smoothing it out. "Happy Bear figgered the boy needed a ride. He figgered right."

"But why?" I asked.

"Like I said, child needed a horse."

"And just like that, he gives up his horse?"

"Yep."

I was fit to be tied. Didn't make no sense. A free horse. And for a child. What was wrong with these people. Heathens. I decided that it was no doubt an attempt to corrupt his young mind and trick him into trusting the savages. It was a fine-looking animal, though. She was a black and white paint with a piebald face. I walked around her. "Good legs," I said. I opened her mouth and looked at her teeth. "Not too old neither."

"She's beautiful," Jake said.

"I wouldn't say all that," I said. "Beautiful is a pretty big word to be tossin' around about a horse."

Bubba dropped his saddle down onto his mule's back. He spoke without regarding me. "Best get yourself ready to travel."

"Jake," I said, "you're gonna need you some leather under your fanny."

"The blanket will be enough," Bubba said. "Blanket was enough for Happy Bear."

"Boy ain't got Injun hide," I said. "Listen, boy, my saddle is especially cut for the back of my horse, but if you want a saddle to ride on, I'll be happy to . . . "

"No," Bubba said.

"No what?"

"No, he ain't gonna trade horses with you."

Jake caught on. "No, I want my horse," he complained and clung to the animal's neck. "She's mine."

"That's right," Bubba said.

"Well, fine," I said. "I was just trying to look out for the boy's comfort, stop his butt from blisterin' and keep him

64

from growin' up deformed and winding up in one of them traveling shows what's got a lady with a beard."

"Child's butt will be fine," Bubba said. "Get saddled up. Trails don't last long in the dust."

While I pulled the cinches of my saddle tight under my horse, I watched Bubba give Jake a boot up onto his mare. The boy sat up there on that Injun blanket like he thought he was a prince or something. There was a real softness in his face, and he didn't look nothing like the wild critter what bit my leg outside the livery.

"You give your horse a name yet?" I asked.

"Yep."

"Well?"

"Well, what?"

"What's her name?"

"It's a secret."

"To hell with both of you Injun-lovin' bastards," I said and climbed into my saddle.

We rode out of camp and continued in the direction we'd been traveling the day before. The sun was just starting to come up, and I was awaiting it eagerly because I thought it might burn some of the chill out of the air.

Finally, the day was on full, but it wasn't until mid-morning that the edge of the chill was gone and then it was replaced by the blunt hammering of the sun's heat. Bubba was grousing that the trail was fading. The ground was becoming more rocky, he said. We wandered without sure signs for a couple of miles and we came onto a water hole where we paused to fill our canteens. Bubba walked around the area and finally kicked up some dust.

"If'n they was here, I can't tell," he said. "I suppose they could have missed the water."

"You mean to tell me you lost them?" I said.

"Not sure." He pulled his mule away from the water and mounted. "Where's Jake?"

I was standing by the black man's mule, holding the reins of my horse and the paint. "Went off into them rocks." I thought about that. "Bubba, you notice how that boy don't never piddle in front of us? He's always trottin' off outa sight to relieve hisself."

"Come on, child," Bubba called out.

"That's a strange boy, I tell you. Why, when I first met him, he barked like a dog and actually bit my leg. Did I tell about that? It was scary."

"No tell."

"Just like a wild boar. I mean, I thought he might have the fever or plague or some such shit."

"Jake!" Bubba called again.

"Coming." The boy came running. "Are we getting closer?" he asked, taking his horse from me and scrambling onto her back.

"The nigger lost 'em," I said.

"Did we lose 'em, Bubba?"

"Seems so," Bubba said.

"So, what now?" I asked, following behind him and the boy as they rode off again toward the west. "I want to know what we do now."

"Try to find the trail again," he said. "It's all we can do."

"I'm not payin' you unless we find 'em," I said.

"We'll find 'em."

We moved on, and before the sun was well into its westward fall, we'd stumbled onto a fresh campsite. I asked Bubba if it was our men and he said he suspected so. When he found a piece of blue flannel and I identified it as a snippet of Sadie's dress, we were sure. Bubba took to studying the place. He knelt by the dead fire, stirred it with a stick, smelled it. He all but shoved his face into the ashes. He roamed from this spot to that spot, feeling the ground, dipping his fingers into dents in the earth. Finally, he stood straight and took in the whole scene.

"Five, maybe six men," he said. "A light foot walked here." He indicated the ground with a point. "Maybe a woman. Prob'ly a woman. She slept here." He moved to the spot. "She walked to where the others slept. No prints come here."

Jake stood at his side, staring at the evidence.

"What are you sayin' about my Sadie?" I asked him.

"I ain't sayin' nothin'. Man, I don't even know your Sadie."

"That's good, cause I ain't payin' you to stand around imaginin' lewd imaginins." I stared at him real hard-like to show him I meant business.

The nigger caught my eyes but wouldn't give 'em up. He said, "Don't get your drawers in a bundle, Marder. You hired me, but you don't own me. Don't nobody own me. You hear what I'm sayin' to you. I ain't no more a slave than you is a child of God."

I looked away to the points of the campsite which he had studied. "So, what now? What do we do now?" I asked. "This is all fine and well, you tellin' me where somebody snoozed, but where are they?"

Bubba turned Jake with a hand on his shoulder and nudged him toward the horses. I walked behind them, asking again—

"What now?"

"Same as before, Marder," Bubba said. "This shit ain't hard. All we can do is follow the trail."

I looked at the road, rutted from wagon wheels. "Where does this road go? You know?"

"Goes to the town of Cahoots."

"You think they're in Cahoots?"

Bubba shrugged. "Road goes there." He dipped into his saddle bag and came out with some jerky. He handed a stick to Jake and tossed one to me.

We followed the road for some miles and dusk started to settle on us and make things hard to see. The dust of the trail was getting into my nose and making me damn uncomfortable. I watched the rhythm of the mare's ass swishing its tail from side to side. I was getting sleepy and wondering if it wasn't about time for us to be stopping for the night, but there seemed to be no pause in the black man.

Then he pulled up short and put out an open hand, which stopped me and the boy and made us be still.

"What you hearin'?" I asked him, straining my ears against the night.

He didn't say nothing, just stepped on slowly down the lane. Then I could hear it too. Voices. Way off-like.

"Is it them?" I asked.

"Shhhh."

My heart was a-racing, and I felt a gnawing in the pit of my belly. I didn't expect results from our efforts so soon. I was prepared for a more protracted search. A couple of lights appeared and moved about in the dense gray before the washed-pink sunset sky.

"Your Sadie wear parfume?" Bubba asked me in a whisper.

"Parfume?"

"You know, that smelly water."

"Hell, no. She's a ranch woman. What in the world would she be wearin' that for?"

"Shhhh."

"You better quit your shushin' me, boy." I felt funny I'd called him a boy, but it just came out.

Bubba climbed down off his mule and handed the reins to Jake. "Stay here," he said, then he looked at me. "The both of you. Stay here and keep quiet. I ain't lookin' to get myself shot up."

"How long should we wait for?" I asked.

"Till I come back or call you."

"What if'n you don't come back?"

I couldn't the see the expression on his face, but I felt it. He walked off into the dark. Some yards away, he hunched over and scooted off the road.

We waited. Bats came out and whispered their wings in the air just above us. I squeezed my head in between my shoulders a little.

"You scared?" Jake asked me.

"Naw, I ain't scared." I tried to spit into dust. "Bubba's the tracker. It's his job to be scurryin' off into the pitch dark night to assess the possible dangers that might lurk about. Especially at night."

"How come?" the boy asked.

"He's got built-in camouflage, that's why. That's a Frenchman's word. Means black as night. I tell you, if'n I was as black as that nigger, I could sneak in close enough to smell their breath and they wouldn't know I was there.

69

But then, I'd be a nigger and prob'ly be so damn sad I'd break into one of them spirituals and give myself away."

"Red Elk said the men we're lookin' for are devils."

I looked at the boy and shook my head. "Forget what you heard them heathens say, boy. They ain't got no god, so what can they know 'bout devils. You need a good god before you can talk about demons and such as that."

The boy leaned forward, staring anxiously into the darkness, absently stroking the mane of his horse.

My horse snorted and spooked at a sudden sound.

9

"GOLL DANG, BUBBA, YOU damn near made my heart go boom, sneakin' up like that. Didn't your ma teach you better'n to be doin' that? I could have drawed my gun and let you have it right betwixt the eyes." I slid down off my horse. "See, boy," I said to Jake. "Couldn't see him at all out here in the black night. Just like a phantom."

"Is it them?" Jake asked.

"Nope. It's a stagecoach what done thrown a wheel. Couple fellas workin' on it and a buncha women runnin' round in big dresses."

"Women?"

"Three of 'em."

"Is they pretty?" I asked.

"Cain't say."

"What do you mean you cain't say? You saw 'em, didn't you?"

"Yeah, I saw 'em, but I cain't say."

"Did you talk to 'em?"

"Nope. Didn't see no point in gettin' shot."

"Well, let's go help 'em," I said.

"Driver and another man are fixin' the wheel awright," Bubba said.

"I'm the boss and I says where we go and when, and I says we're goin' out there to offer assistance to them good, white, god-fearin' people."

"Whatever," Bubba said. "But lallygaggin' with them folks ain't gonna get us no closer to your Sadie."

"We'll make up the gap tomorrow." I looked at the boy and then at Bubba again. "Let's ride on. C'mon."

We moved through the night toward the torches. Soon I could hear the voices more clearly, being able to make out the delicate sopranie of female women. My spirits lifted considerable, and I found my nose feeling the night air for the sweet aroma Bubba had reported.

"Yo there!" a man with an orange-glowing torch called from the stagecoach.

"You be needin' help?" I asked.

I could see the man lower the rifle he held in one hand. "Another strong shoulder would be of use."

We wandered full into the glow of the torches. The flickering light bothered my eyes. "My name is Marder," I announced.

"Simms," the man in the driver's coat said, stepping to me as I dismounted. I shook his hand while he glanced over at Bubba and the boy. "We sure enough could use some extra muscle."

"Bubba," I said, "get over there and measure up the situation and see what you can do to help out Mr. Simms." I heard the nigger grumble something as he fell out of his saddle and landed loud on his feet. "My hired boy," I said to Simms, "will get you straight in no time."

"Much obliged." Simms followed Bubba to the stage.

The women stepped forward, three of them, the light of the torch held by the second man behind them making it hard to see their faces clear. Just a glimpse of those flowing skirts, though, was exciting, and my eyes strained to find their features.

"Are we ever glad to see you," one woman said. Closer, I could see her face, all painted like a picture and sitting beneath a tall head of hair.

"His boy'll have us goin' in no time," the driver said over his shoulder.

I turned to Jake. "Go see if you can help Bubba." I watched as he got down and tied his horse to a shrub. "But don't you be gettin' in the way now."

"I'm Loretta," the first woman said.

"My name's Marder, missy, Curt Marder."

"Pleased to make your acquaintance." She held her skirt out and kinda dipped. "This here is Fannie and this here is Roberta. Gals, this is Dirt Martin."

"That's Curt Marder," I said.

"Where?" asked Fannie, looking around and I knew she was the dumb one.

"Me, I'm Curt Marder."

"Call me Bobby," said the little one. "My name is Roberta, but I go by Bobby 'cause I like it better. My mama calls me Bobby. You can too. I go by Bobby, just like you go by Curt, Dirt."

"No, little lady, my name is Curt."

Bobby had a big smile and she used it, then said, "I wouldn't want to be called Dirt either."

"Is that your child?" Fannie asked, turning to observe the boy.

"No."

"Does the darkie work for you?" Loretta asked.

"Yes, missy, he does."

The second man pushed through the females to me and stuck out his hand. "I want to thank you personal for yer Christian charity, my good man. I'm Simon Phrensie."

I shook his hand. "Curt, *Curt* Marder."

"Pleased to meet you, Curt-*curt*. That is the accent on the second syllable? What kinda name is that? Makes no never mind. I'm a man of the cloth, of God, and what's more, I'm a vendor of bibles. Nice bibles, son, hardly used and with most of their pages. Tell me, are you in need of a copy of the Good Book? The word of the Almighty weighs little but means so much."

"Where you folks headed?" I asked.

"Cahoots," said Loretta.

Phrensie cleared his throat. "Cahoots is gettin' the railroad. God save the people. There should be plenty of work there for a man like myself. Sin is the close companion of progress, brother. I mean, word of the railroad is just out and look at the cargo that today travels with me."

"Hey, we ain't sin," Loretta said.

"You ain't sin precisely," Phrensie said, "but you are women, and as such you are the cause of sin, lest I remind you of the story of Adam and Eve. You women are not only the keys but the doorway to damnation and eternal hell."

"Oh yeah," Fannie said.

"It's in the Bible, and I'm more than happy to make you a good price." Phrensie turned to me and handed me the bible he was holding. "Take this, my friend. It has most of its pages, like I said. A bout with illness just as we pulled away from Kansas City saw the demise of most of Deuteronomy. Ever been to Kansas City?"

"Cain't say that I have."

"A whole city of sin, brother. Gamblin', fast women, drinkin' and fightin'."

"I'm from Kansas City," Fannie said.

"My point is made," Phrensie said.

"What do you mean by that?" Fannie raised her voice.

"I've had just about enough outa you, preacher man," Loretta said, shaking her fist. "Ever since we got on board, you been jawin' at us and rubbin' up against us when we fall asleep."

"Lies," Phrensie said.

"It's true and you know it," Bobby said. "You been scraping your thighs agin me every chance you git."

"You women should read the Good Book."

"You should read a good book, yerself," Fannie said.

"The Bible tells us that it is a sin against God to bear false witness."

"Ain't it a sin to rub up agin ladies?" Bobby asked.

"We should all read the Bible."

I looked at the bible in my hand. "I don't have to read this now, do I?"

"Read it at your leisure, brother. Take your time and savor it, enjoy it, let it into your heart. A two-bit donation would not be out of order at this moment."

Loretta pushed Phrensie aside. Out of my saddle, I was standing close to her. "You smell awful nice, ma'am."

"You know, you're kinda cute," she said.

I saw Fannie and Bobby wander off toward where Bubba and the driver were working on the wheel.

"Cute?" I said.

"Yeah. And you must have a lot of money to be travelin' round with a hired man."

"Oh, I do awright." I looked at her big eyes shining there in the dark. "What you gals gonna do in Cahoots?"

"We're workin' gals."

"Are you singers?"

"Yeah, darlin'."

"I like singin'."

"Well, you stick close to me for a while, honey, and you'll hear some singin', if'n you know what I mean. You do know what I mean?"

"Hot damn."

Phrensie was just standing by, holding his torch and watching us talk. "Oh, brother," he said, "don't let this harlot ruin your entry into the kingdom of the Almighty."

"We need some weight here," the driver called out.

Fannie was now holding the driver's torch. Simms, Bobby and Jake were pressing their bodies down on a skinny tree laid over a pile of rocks and stuck under the stage. They were straining to lift the coach so Bubba could set the wheel. Phrensie passed his torch to Loretta and threw in his chubby gut. Loretta and I watched while the wheel got placed and the pin hammered in. A cheer went up into the night. The driver slapped Bubba's back. Fannie and Bobby danced around a bit, the skirts bouncing shadows against the ground. They grabbed Jake and twirled him betwixt them. Word got around that the nigger's name was Bubba, and then they was all thanking him.

"Yer welcome," I said. "Good work, Bubba."

Loretta came back to me and slipped her arm through mine. "You just wait till we get to Cahoots. I am gonna show you a *good* time."

"Okay, ladies," Simms said. "Just another couple of hours to Cahoots."

76

"And the night's young," Loretta said.

Bobby and Fannie were making a fuss over Jake, touching his hair and giggling.

"Are you comin' to town with us, Dirt?" Bobby asked.

"That's Curt," I told her. "Yeah, I reckon we could all use a little trip into town. Bubba, I think you'd like that, wouldn't you?"

"Cain't live without it."

"And he's gonna ride in the stage with us," Loretta said, blowing in my ear. "There's plenty room if'n you don't mind being squeezed in *real* tight."

"Oh, I don't mind," I said. "Bubba, we're goin' into town with these good folks. So, mount up. Jake, you bring my horse along. I'm ridin' with the ladies."

Simms called to Bubba. "You and the child can ride on top with me. Just tie your animals to the back and climb up."

"How long you folks been travelin'?" I asked, helping Fannie up into the box.

"Ten days," Phrensie said.

Ten days, I thought, squishing myself in between Fannie and Loretta. Bobby and the preacher were sitting across from me with some distance between them. Ten days of no bathing. I smelled bad enough, but at least it was me. The stench of the passengers and the swelling waves of perfume left me dizzy. And it was hot inside, despite the cooling night, even with the flaps of the windows rolled open on both sides. The motion of the stage lacked any rhythm and the jostling defied anticipation. With all the rocking and creaking, conversation was near impossible. Our bodies were tossed about. The women were soft enough to land on, but they did stink. Bobby was sitting directly in front of me, smiling her young smile without rest. I grinned back at her until my face ached, and then I realized that she was sound asleep with that horseshoe frozen on her lips.

10

I'D HAD LITTLE TRUCK with god and the Bible and like that, and maybe I didn't know much, but everything that Simon Phrensie and every other scripture vulture on the plains called sin was what I thought a man was supposed to sniff out. I could see as we rolled onto the main thoroughfare of Cahoots that there was plenty of sniffing to do. There was men shooting every which way into the night sky, hugging on women outside what I took to be an ill-repute house and lots of drunken singing and staggering about. Bobby and Fannie were pressed up to the windows, smiling and pointing and getting pointed at. Loretta was snuggled up to me talking all sorts of nonsense about clean sheets and soft pillows. The stage pulled up in front of the office and we fell out into the cool, dusty street. Bubba and Jake were already down and untying our animals.

"Well, here we are, safe and sound," the driver said.

"Praise the Lord," said Phrensie.

I glanced behind to see Bobby handing a lacy hanky to Jake. It struck me funny. I watched him sniff the thing, but I didn't say nothing about it.

Loretta was all plastered up against me again. "You gonna come with me, sugar?"

The invitation was welcome and, I thought, appropriate, but I was immediately reminded by the lightness of my trousers of the emptiness in my pockets. I'd have to talk Bubba out of a bit of the money I knew he had before I could buy a couple of whiskeys and remain in good standing with Loretta.

"You wander on and I'll catch up with you later," I said. "I gotta get my hired help and the child squared away before I can do anything else. You know, business before pleasure and all that."

"Okay, cutie," she said, planting a big red kiss on my cheek. "But you hurry up now. I'll be waitin' over at the Silver Dollar. And remember, pleasure is my business."

"The Silver Dollar," I said to let her know I was committing it to memory. "I'll be over directly."

She gave me a big wink and stepped away to join the other women.

Phrensie let drop a box handed to him from the roof of the stagecoach, then turned to me. "You can go find her later if you want, but if I was you, I'd be investin' my money in a couple of King Jameses. Buy two, better three, and you can be sure you got all the pages. You know what man has got that other animals don't?"

"What's that?"

"Man has an insufferably cruel god to look up to."

I looked at the box at his feet. "I don't need a bible."

"You say that now."

I stepped away from him.

Bubba had his mule in tow. He looked at me and said, "Me and Jake is goin' over to the livery."

"I'll go with you to make sure things get all situated proper-like."

"Suit yerself."

"I thought the two of you might feel more comfortable if'n I was with you till you got settled in."

"Awright," Bubba said.

"Awright what?"

"Just awright."

I walked behind them. The boy held the reins to his paint and my horse. A couple of shots rang out and I looked up the street to see a couple of cowpokes tossing coins in the air to shoot in the torch light.

"You know, somebody in this town might be able to help us," I said.

"Prob'ly," Bubba said.

"I mean, maybe somebody'll know where the sidewinders we's lookin' for are holed up or which way they went or some such stuff as that."

"Could be."

We got to the livery and they tied the animals to the post outside. A crowd of horses in the corral behind the stables stamped feet and snorted. Bubba and Jake began to undo the saddles. Bubba whistled some familiar tune that immediately stepped on my nerves.

"I might need to pay something for that information that might be so helpful to us," I said. "That somebody who knows that something ain't bound to give it up for free."

"I ain't got no objections," Bubba said. He tossed his saddle onto the shoulder-high fence of the pen behind him, then took my saddle from Jake and put it there too.

81

"Wouldn't matter none if'n you did have some kind of objection," I said.

"I s'pose not."

"I reckon I should come out with what it is I want to ask you." I felt my belly turning sideways again.

"Might help some."

"Nigger, I need some money."

He didn't let on that my choice of words bothered him. He said, "I ain't got no doubt."

"I'm sorry I called you a nigger," I said.

"I'll study that notion for a spell."

"Do you have any money?" I asked.

"I reckon I got a little on me. I also reckon it ain't wise to go round announcin' it to folks."

"Give me some."

"Marder, you already owe me for the supplies," he said.

"Well, that is true, Bubba, but that's beans under the bridge. It's done. Now, just give me a dollar."

The black man looked at me, then at the boy with a kind of frowning smile. He dug into the side pocket of his vest and came out with a coin which he flipped through the air to me.

"That's another dollar you owe me. I'll be writin' it down later."

I gave the coin a breath and rubbed it with my thumb. "You do that."

Jake and Bubba were headed into the barn of the livery with their bedrolls, and Jake was sniffing that hanky that Bobby had given him.

"What's with that rag?" I asked.

"That lady just gave it to me."

"I guess that was nice of her." I watched their backs. "I

mean, she coulda given you a bible or somethin'. Right?" They turned the corner out of sight. "I'll see you two in the mornin'."

There were actually a couple of saloons on the big street of Cahoots, facing each other, all lit up, but somehow not seeming to fight. I reckon there was so much wildness to go around that nobody was hurting. The High Hog was the tavern that caught my initial fancy. I liked the blue color of the swinging doors, to tell the good Lord's honest truth, and plus there was a soft spot in my heart for hogs, despite some vague memory of a brother falling into a pen and being eaten by some. I reckon I was young or not terribly taken with that brother.

But it was the Silver Dollar I chose to enter, the name of it having been spoken into my ear by the painted lips of pining Loretta. It didn't have swinging doors, but it had stained glass like in a church in the front windows. I walked in and there was no pause in anybody's carryings on. The place was teeming with folks, especially around the bar, where they was like ants at a piece of rock candy. I made my way through the well-lighted room toward the whiskey. On my way I spied and was spied by Simms, the stagecoach driver.

A few whiskeys down his gullet had made his voice louder, and he said, without timidity, "And here is the man who saved us a night out in the wild at the mercy of whatever savages or wild beasts was lurkin' about. Boys, I'd like you to give a hearty Cahoots salute to Dirt Martin."

What followed was my getting knocked silly by palms to the back from people who were familiar by smell only.

"Good feller, Dirt," I heard.

"Atta cowboy."

"What kinda name is Dirt?"

"Yup," Simms said. "He showed up with his hired man and got us straight faster than a scared deer shits."

Next thing I knew, fellas was buying me drinks and smiling at me and my belly was getting warm and cozy and loose. The dollar that Bubba had given me stopped trying to burn its way through my britches and I just leaned against the bar and put the whiskey down as fast as the barkeep could pour it. The Silver Dollar was a fine place. They had little bowls out on the bar filled with pecans from back east just waiting for a fella to crack them open. The floor was lousy with nutshells that crunched underfoot.

Some time slipped by and my mind turned to Loretta and I wondered where she was. I leaned in to the bartender and asked, "You seen a woman all painted up around here?"

"All the women round here is painted up," he said.

"I mean them three what just come into town on the stage. You seen them?"

He smiled. "I seen 'em. Pretty, ain't they. They took rooms upstairs. I don't know which rooms. I just tend this here bar. I got no truck with the rooms and the women."

Just about then I heard my name tethered to Loretta's voice. "Dirt! Dirt!" Well, it was kinda my name. She was halfway down the stairs in a clean dress, waving to me, only me.

Men nearby gave me a rutting look.

I waved back to her. I didn't move from my place at the bar. I stayed bellied up and watched her in the mirror as she weaved her way through the reaching and groping hands toward me. She laughed, slapping away the advances.

I turned as she reached me and she threw her arms around me and hugged tight. She left red paint on my face, I'm sure. She was soft and full under all them clean ruffles of clothes and smelled of sweet water.

"I'm so glad to see you, sugar," she said and offered a quick but disinterested glance at the man on her other side.

"I'm glad to see you, too," I said.

"So, you gonna buy a gal a drink?" She took the empty glass from my hand and set it loudly on the bar.

I took the dollar from my pocket in a way to suggest that it had company in my britches—I looked at it like I wanted to know just what it was. "Whiskey?" I asked her.

She nodded.

"Two whiskeys," I called to the barkeep.

The drinks were delivered and we tossed them down. She smiled at me and teased the rim of her glass with her tongue. "I'm thinkin' it's awfully noisy in here," she said.

"What?"

"I said I think we should go upstairs." She looked into my eyes. "I want to show you my room."

"What for?"

"For the rest of what we got to do, hon."

"Well, I s'pose then we ought to get on up them stairs, li'l lady." My knees felt weak and unsteady under me as I pushed away from the bar, but I followed her successfully through the crowd to the stairway. I was about three steps up when a pretty good fight began to burn through the room. It was serious for the two fellas what started it, but a high ol' rip-snorter for the rest.

At the door to her room, Loretta turned and kissed me

full on the lips. I tasted the paint and didn't like it, but I forged on in the pioneer spirit. We pressed through the door and into her chamber. It was lighted yellow by the glow of a lantern on her night table. She pulled me to the bed and down on top of her, laughing all the way. By now I was liking the taste of the paint, and through the haze of my drunkenness I felt a stirring.

"Are we gonna do it up right?" she asked.

"I reckon so," I said.

"You want to pay as you go, or you want I should run a tab for you?"

"Pardon?"

"How you want to pay?"

"Pay?" I asked.

"I already done told you I'm a workin' gal," she said, smiling big.

I was taken with sudden appreciation of my intoxication because it allowed me to forgo the feeling of embarrassment that I felt compelled to consider.

"I gotta tell you somethin', Loretta."

She pushed me off her and sat up, raised a hand to her hair. I sat up, too, and looked at the door and then the window.

"What?" she asked.

"I ain't got no money."

I don't know what she hit me with, but it hurt like hell. The whiskey absorbed a lot of the pain, but still I didn't much care for being punched on, and she just wouldn't let up. I tried to get to the door, but the shattering of the washing bowl against it steered me toward the window. She kept on coming at me and I kept on backing up, until I felt the open window behind me. I lost my balance and tumbled butt first out onto the roof. Loretta didn't chase me out there but leaned out into the dark, yelling things about me that were just awful and giving up private things to the night like she's been talking to my wife.

Loretta was so frightening that my fear of high places temporarily vanished and I scurried across that roof quicker than a lizard on a hot rock. I rounded the corner to the front of the saloon and found myself sliding down toward the edge. I kept sliding and slid right on off, landing on my behind in the street between two tied horses and just shy of a cedar hitching post. I gained my legs, rubbed my hindy and then remembered Loretta and decided to run away from there pronto. Drunk as I was, it wasn't clear to me in which direction lay the livery. I wandered around for a bit, bumping into other inebriated cowboys here and stepping over folks sleeping in the street there.

The smells and sounds of stock finally pulled me toward the livery. As I walked to the barn door, I could hear a ruckus from inside. I cracked open the door, and there, in the dim light of a candle in the far corner, was a fight. A steadied look told me it was Bubba, and he was fighting a white man and giving him a trouncing too. He pulled that black fist back and give it to the white man like he was white hisself. Then the man was sitting in a stack of hay nursing his bloody mouth with a forearm. Bubba left off and turned away.

The white man slid his pistol out of his pocket and aimed it at Bubba's back. I wanted to yell something, but I didn't know what. My fear sharpened my vision and I could see his finger squeezing that trigger clear as anything.

The report was startling even though I knew it was coming. But Bubba didn't drop. In fact, he turned to face the white man. I looked at him, too, and saw that he slumped over and that his shirt was slowly darkening.

I glanced around and there was Jake, holding Bubba's gun in his lap. His little body was shaking something awful. Bubba went to him and was on his knees, hugging him and talking soft.

"Have mercy," I said, running to the shot man and then to the two of them.

"Is he dead?" Bubba asked.

"I don't know," I said.

"Take care here," he said.

I knelt down beside Jake while Bubba went across the room. I watched as he touched the man.

"He's dead," Bubba said. "Get the boy together and I'll saddle the horses."

"What happened?" I asked.

"Just get the boy ready to travel." Bubba started outside.

I jumped up and grabbed him. "What happened? Bubba, tell me what happened."

"Jake just shot that man." He pointed.

"I ain't stupid."

"He's white and I'm black and I was fightin' him and two-hundred white witnesses cain't convince the twelve I'll never see that I didn't kill him."

"Why was you fightin' him?" I asked.

Bubba stopped, and for the first time his face softened. He said, "He was trying to rape Jake."

"He what?"

"He was trying to rape Jake. I went out to relieve myself, and when I come back, he was in here."

"Trying to rape a boy?"

"Marder, such a thing is possible, but Jake happens to be a girl."

"A girl?"

"Now, with or without you, me and Jake is gettin' the hell outa here. I ain't gettin' lynched by nobody."

"Awright, Bubba."

"You get the child. I'll get the horses."

11

THE WARMTH THAT THE alcohol had once offered my empty belly was gone and I shivered like an aspen leaf in the dark early morning hours. The chill and my sore, aching, tired fanny bone against the saddle worked to sober me up some, and I began to recall the previous hours. I said out loud to no one in particular, "Oh shit."

"Yep," Bubba said.

Jake looked much smaller now, folded up in Bubba's lap on the mule. I had Jake's paint tethered to the horn of my saddle. I couldn't tell if the child was asleep. Her eyes was open, but she weren't blinking none.

"Bubba," I said. "Why don't we stop and build us a fire. It's colder than a dead man's dick out here. We could warm up the little one."

"I reckon we'll keep on movin'."

"Movin' to where? They ain't gonna hang no kid, 'specially no girl, for shootin' some drunk snake turd what's tryin' to violate her improper-like."

"Marder, I don't mean to sound like I'm thinkin' about myself, but that's what I'm doin'. I'm the one they gonna string up."

"String up? Ain't nobody gonna string nobody up 'cause

didn't nobody see what happened. All they is gonna find is one dead cowpoke."

"How many black men did you see in that town back there?" Bubba asked.

I thought. "Well, none, 'ceptin' you."

"And how many folks you reckon saw me?" he asked. "Not countin' the ones that yelled nigger at me." He didn't wait for an answer. "They all saw me, stared at me, wantin' in their hearts for me to mess up in some kinda, any kinda way."

I didn't say nothing, just remembered times when I'd seen niggers in the street and felt just the way he was describing, like they was entertainment just waiting to happen.

"So, where we goin'?" I asked.

"Someplace safe."

"Where's that?"

"We're goin' to the Indian camp."

"The Injun camp? Easter bunny, man. We can't be ridin' into some heathen village just like that." I let out a breath. "You mean you know where they is? Soldiers been scourin' the territory for 'em."

"That's where we're goin'. You're welcome to fall away any time."

There was no talking sense to the black man, so I let my voice rest. Thoughts of all them red men got my heart to jigging and my blood to coursing and I warmed up a mite. I figgered I'd just hang close to Bubba, do as he did and pray a lot. I'd learned my frontier Christian lessons well — lie, steal, cheat, and, when all that failed, pray.

It was daybreak when we hauled our spent bodies the last yards toward the dreaded Injun camp. I was too scared to be cold, and I was confused as Bubba released a sigh of relief. A couple of braves spotted us and came walking in our direction. They was armed with rifles.

"Bubba, do they know we're friendly?" I asked.

"Are we friendly?" he asked me.

"Huh?"

"I don't know what they know," he said. "Cain't say I ever seen them two before."

"Shouldn't you say somethin'?"

"No, I don't think so. I ain't so good with their tongue, and they might get the wrong idea and shoot you."

I made up my mind to keep quiet. The camp was set on the bank of a river. Big cottonwoods crowded toward the water and lupines climbed purple up the slope behind on the other side. Their tepees was spread out evenly, and smoke spiraled up from six or seven fires.

The approaching Injuns spoke when they was ten yards away, and to my surprise they spoke English and said, "You must be the man they call Bubba."

"I am," Bubba said.

"Big Elk has spoken of you. He says you are to be trusted." The speaking one looked at me.

"His name is Marder," Bubba said.

He looked at me again, raised his hand and said, "How."

The two braves laughed, then let off. The same one spoke. "Is the small one hurt?"

"She needs rest," Bubba said. "We need a place to hide."

"You are welcome here. Big Elk and Happy Bear will be back soon from the hunt." With that they turned and walked back toward the tepees.

Bubba gave his mule a light nudge and we followed them.

Squaws came running out to meet us. They took Jake from Bubba and carried her into one of the tepees.

Bubba watched until she was out of sight. He spoke to me without a glance. "Best go warm yourself by a fire. Any of 'em will do. These folks won't bother you. Try treatin' them like you would treat white folks—no, like you wanna be treated. Try that."

Bubba's eyes was real tired-looking and I found myself feeling kinda sad for him. I dismounted by a fire site and watched the black man step away toward the river with his mule, my horse and Jake's spotted pony in tow. At the fire was an old man sitting under a blanket, a little pile of sticks beside him. He opened his eyes and regarded me for only a second.

"Hello," I said. I sat across from him and showed my palms the flames. The heat felt good.

I sat there going over it all again. If I had let emotion have its sway, I'd have been screaming my fool head off and them Injuns would have come out of everywhere to tie me down so I wouldn't be giving away the location of their camp. But I held it in and let it spin me quietly. Jake was a girl. Didn't that beat all. Some things began to make sense, like her size and her sneaky piddling. I was briefly mad at Bubba for not letting on, especially since he knew I thought she was a he. He just let me make a fool out of myself.

I could see his mule and the other horses at the water's edge, but I'd lost sight of him. I'd lost sight of a whole lot. My ranch. My wife. And now probably my mission of revenge and getting back my woman. I studied the closed eyes of the old man and felt myself drifting toward sleep.

I had me one of them real deep drunken sleeps what's got no dreams and breaks hard. My rest was cracked by smoke and I figured the old man had tossed on a couple of green sticks. I opened my eyes and saw faces through a veil of smoke. I realized that not only was I not sitting, but I wasn't exactly standing neither and I contemplated throwing a fit, but that's better done when your hands ain't tied behind your back and your back ain't tied to a stake. The heathens was standing all around me, grinning through gaudy face paint. At my feet was a pile of wood working itself up to a blaze. I did what nature and my good mama taught me. I screamed.

Then I was yelling for Bubba. The more I yelled, the more the Injuns smiled, until I was hoarse and they was laughing. I focused on the face of Big Elk. He was a-laughing so hard he was crying. The smoke burned my eyes something awful, and I knew it looked like I was crying too. I stopped my shouting and prayed.

"God," I said, out loud because my mama told me that worked better. "Please don't let these godless bastards cook me up like a razorback from Arkysaw. I'm sorry for all my misdeeds and transgressions, such as lyin', and cheatin' and unclean language . . . "

I lost my line of thought because Big Elk and some others were now rolling around on the ground howling and holding their sides. The laughter wound slowly down, and to my surprise, and near horror, the kindling sticks of the fire were getting kicked away.

The smoke cleared and I saw Bubba with Happy Bear. The black man showed a slight smile, and he pointed in such a way that I knew he was telling them to cut me loose.

"Thank you, Jesus God oh lordy," I said as a boy sawed through the ropes at my feet and hands. I rubbed my wrists and stepped over the smoldering twigs toward Bubba.

"What in the dag-nabbed world is goin' on here, Bubba?" I asked.

"What are you talkin' about?" he asked me.

"Talkin' about? Talkin' about? These friends of yourn just tried to roast me alive like a side of beef."

"They wasn't really gonna hurt you, Marder," the black man said. "They was just tryin' to cheer me up a bit." He nodded to Big Elk. "It was just a joke."

"A joke?"

"Yeah, just a little funny," the nigger said.

"A little funny? Man, I was scared out of my free white mind tied up there like that."

"I reckon so," he said, staring at my face.

Big Elk, Happy Bear and the other braves laughed again.

"To hell with all of you," I said and marched away toward the river. I smelled of wood smoke and I was hot under the collar. I'm telling you I was steamed. I got to the water and splashed a couple of handfuls onto my face, then paused to regard my reflection. Well, I felt damn ridiculous. Them heathens had painted me up just like them. I scrubbed it off, none too easily, and decided not to make mention of the offense.

Bubba came and told me that I was welcome to eat from the fire of Happy Bear and Running Dear and he gave a point up the bank.

"Ain't you got nothing to say?" I asked.

He looked at the river and thought. "Bon appetitty?"

"Don't be talkin' Injun to me."

He turned and stepped away and I wandered off toward the fire in the direction he'd pointed. I approached a brave near as big around as Happy Bear. He smiled large and said, "Help yourself to *grub*."

"Thank you kindly." I looked at the meat cooking over the flames. "Tell me, just what kinda critter we got us cookin' here."

"Help yourself to *grub*."

"I will, thank you."

"*Grub*."

I looked around and then at the fat man. "You got a name?"

He just smiled, then tore off a piece of the animal and threw it into his mouth. The smacking of his lips made the food look real good. I took a piece myself. It was tasty, greasy like bear but it weren't near big enough.

Happy Bear came up and nodded, watched me chew, then looked at the meat cooking. "Is that good?" he asked.

"Yep," I said. "What is it? Beaver? Badger? Raccoon?"

He looked at the other Injun, then back at the meat. "We don't know." He offered a shrug. "Only Crazy Scar will eat it." He turned and walked away.

Crazy Scar grinned again. "*Grub*."

12

BUBBA WANDERED OFF WITH Big Elk and the other men to hunt. Leastways, this was what I figured. They didn't invite me along, but I refused to feel slighted, just to spite them. After a couple of days with them Injuns, I would have thought I'd welcome the sight of any white person. But the white face that came riding into camp was Simon Phrensie's. He was driving a buckboard pulled by a pair of white mules. The older squaws were the first to move toward him, then the younger ones, slowly, with quiet talk among themselves. They gathered around the wagon while Phrensie stood on the seat and looked down at them.

"Gather around me, you sweet pagans, and let me make you heathens with the right to enter hell," he said. "The Lord hath sent me." He raised his arms over his head, a Bible in his left hand. "He hath sent me to share with you his word. What is his word, you ask? Where can you findth his word, you ask? In thisth book. I will read from the book of Isaiah." He opened the Bible and read, " 'Every valley shall be exalted, and every mountain and hill shall be made low: and the crooked shall be made straight, and the rough places plain: And the glory of the Lord shall be revealed, and the flesh shall see it together: for the mouth of the Lord hath spoken it.' " He closed the book, then his eyes for a second. "What sayeth ye to that?"

The women looked at each other, then broke out in applause. Phrensie looked surprised.

"Are you telling me you understand what it means?" he asked. He studied their silent faces. "I'll tell you. It means that the white man's god can be something to you, too. He can make mountains flat and deserts wet, but he cannot make you poor red devils white. So, what you need is not one of these overwritten testaments to the existence of a heaven you can never enter, but one of these bottles." He reached down by his feet and held up a clear bottle of light brown liquid. "I guarantee this will get you close to the Almighty."

The squaws looked at one another, nodding and stepping forward.

I moved to the back edge of the crowd, raking sweat from my forehead with the back of my hand. Phrensie spotted me and pointed. "My friend from the stagecoach," he said and climbed down from the buckboard. He walked toward me as the squaws went about their business.

"How is it you come to be here, brother?" he asked.

I looked about, to the river and over my shoulder for Bubba or any of the braves but didn't find them. I saw Jake peek out of the tepee she'd been in since we got there. Looking at her face now, I couldn't believe I ever thought she was a him. I put my eyes back on Phrensie. I didn't have an answer for him.

Then Phrensie spotted Jake's face behind the flap of the tent. "Why do you have this vision of white beauty here with you? Is she your child?"

100

"No."

He held up the bottle in his hand. "I fear I'll have little luck selling my fine and potent elixir here."

"Prob'ly."

"The child is with you, though?"

"I reckon so."

"A young, fresh, white thing like that hadn't ought be so close to these heathen women." Jake's head pulled back into the tepee. "You like whiskey?"

"Course I do."

He handed the bottle to me. "Here then. Take this and we'll just call it good. We're square."

"Square?"

"You know, even."

I figured he was still real grateful for my having effected his rescue on the trail. I said, "Fine by me."

"Enjoy."

I wandered off to do so.

The whiskey didn't have no profound effect, being watered down something terrible, but it was better than river water. I was sitting on the bank wondering how I could pull out a fish for dinner when I heard a commotion from the camp. I got up and walked that way. Bubba and the braves was back. I knew because I saw the black man's mule and a crowd of winded ponies. There was something wrong. The horses were in the middle of the village. The squaws were excited.

"What is it?" I asked an old woman who was running past me toward the river. She didn't answer, didn't so much as pause.

I found Bubba and walked to him.

"Where is Jake?" he asked.

"I guess she's with the squaws."

"She ain't. You didn't see her?"

I shook my head. "I been down by the river. She didn't come down there."

He looked at the empty bottle in my hand. "Where did that bottle come from?"

Before I could answer, Happy Bear was tapping Bubba on the shoulder and talking to him. A squaw was there and she was talking too. The black man listened, then returned to me.

"Simon Phrensie gave it to me," I said. "You remember, that bible drummer from the stage."

"He was here."

"Yep," I said.

"And he just gave that to you."

"Yep."

"For nothing."

"A token of appreciation for gettin' the stagecoach goin'," I said.

Bubba looked at the squaw, at Happy Bear, then at the ground. Without looking at me, he said, "Mount up, Marder. We gotta find Jake."

All saddled up, we rode out of the village and followed the river south.

"Boy, I don't know what you're so worried about," I said. "She's with her own kind now. And a preacher man. He'll take good care of her, you know, give her religion and like that. He'll prob'ly get her into one of them convents and she'll wear one of them long things and learn how to talk French and cook."

Bubba didn't say nothing.

"What good was that female going to be to us anyway? She's too little to pick anything up, and she cain't use a gun. Ain't natural. She already got us—you, she got you into a peck of trouble." I looked at the mountains. I could tell by his silence that he weren't impressed by my argument. "How we gonna catch him?"

"We're gonna split up," he said.

"Split up? You mean, you and me goin' in different directions that ain't the same?"

"Pretty much."

"Well, I have to say that I ain't for certain that's a truly good idear."

"You said it."

I looked at the sky. It would be dark soon. "Maybe we should ride on together just a spell longer, like maybe till morning."

"You keep goin' south along the river here, and I'll cross over and ride west," Bubba said.

"How we gonna meet up again?"

"I'll find you."

"What if he went back to Cahoots?" I asked.

"Me and the braves just come from that direction."

Damn if he didn't have a answer for everything, the know-it-all. I sat and watched him march his mule across the river. He hit a hole about halfway but pushed on through. He didn't so much as offer a wave from the other side.

13

IT WASN'T CLEAR TO me just what was to be done if I caught up to Phrensie and the girl. Sure, deep down I had a bad feeling about Jake being with the preacher, but I had my own problems. I wasn't no kin to the kid.

I stopped before it was too dark and built a little fire to warm up by. Heating up my bones, I was kinda surprised at how I missed the safety of the Indian village. I never was partial to the night hours back home, but here in the high country, where it got colder and even darker, the night seemed filled with more dangers. A lacy chill decorated my spine as coyotes sang bloody songs down river. My education might have been (as some fancy pants in Virginia City once put it) *slender*, but I knew when to be scared.

I laid out my roll and snuggled down for what I suspected would be an unsatisfying and ill-advised sleep.

A real bad smell woke me up. It was a poor way to find consciousness. I could feel sunlight on the other side of my eyelids, but I kept them closed and tried to fan the stench off onto a passing breeze. It stayed though, and boy howdy, was it god-awful.

"Yuk, yuk, yuk," I heard and opened my eyes. The

voice was deep and raspy, like it was coming through a seine. The words fell from a face that wore a filthy, matted red beard, smiling nasty and brown. Behind him were two similar faces, none the more attractive for the company. I slid a hand down my side, feeling for my gun, but it weren't there.

"Howdy?" I said.

"Yuk, yuk, yuk." This from one of the uglies in the rear.

A breeze pushed from behind them and I gagged out a smile.

"Yuk, yuk, yuk."

"Is that all you boys can say? 'Yuk, yuk?' " They just smiled at me. "My name is Marder. What's yourn?" I stuck out my hand to shake.

One of the stinking beaver turds had actually built a fire and had a pot of coffee cooking. I could scarcely smell the brew under the roar of their stench.

"Yuk, yuk, yuk."

They sat around the fire and now seemed to ignore me. They looked cozy there, nursing their mugs, nestled in their cloud of filth. They didn't talk to each other. It wasn't apparent they could. I stood up and knocked the dirt off my knees and seat and said nothing. I brushed a hand against my empty holster. Still, they didn't look at me. I took a little backward step in the direction of my horse.

"Yuk, yuk, yuk." One of them—the three of them was twins, I swear—gained his feet and walked over to me. "Yuk, yuk, yuk," he said to my face and his breath damn near killed me. It smelled like rotting figs, a thin, metallic stink which wrapped around my head and sapped the strength right out of me. I felt my knees buckle.

"Whoa," I said. "What you cowpokes been eatin'? Hey,

I'm just tryin' to be friendly. You fellas wanna be friendly, don't you?"

"Yuk, yuk, yuk."

"Mind if I have a little of your coffee there?" I moved over and sat at the fire with the other two. I leaned over and smelled the pot. "Smells real good."

One of them handed me his tin mug. I didn't want to touch it, but fear pressed me on. The coffee tasted pretty okay if I didn't breathe. "Good," I said.

I looked at the sun. "Well, diddle me proper," I said. "Looky at how the time is scootin' by. And me with this real important appointment in town with my trigger-happy brother the sheriff." I stood up. "So, I reckon I'll be seein' you boys around. Been nice visitin' with you. Thanks for the coffee. And the sparklin' conversation. Sterlin', I tell you, just sterlin'."

They stood with me, and it was plain that my leavin' was not in the plan.

"What do you want from me?"

Then they was all yuk, yuk, yukkin', and one of them went over to their pack horse, untied a shovel and come back with it. He dropped it at my feet.

"What's this for? Listen, boys, I like fun just as much as the next fella."

"Yuk, yuk, yuk," from all of them.

"I take it you want me to dig," I said and bent to pick up the shovel. I considered swinging the tool and clocking the nearest one of them, but a pistol was drawn and I took this as an affirmative response to my query about excavation.

I put the blade of the shovel to the soil and pressed it

down with my boot. I smiled at them and tossed a scoop off to the side. "How deep you want me to dig?"

The sun was past straight up and slipping west and I was still digging. I was standing in a shoulder-deep hole that was approaching the dreaded six feet. It weren't no grave, unless they was planning on putting me in upright.

Dusk was coming on and I was well into my second hole. My muscles ached something awful. This second was much larger than the first. It was much too large to be my final resting place. I just kept digging.

"Yuk, yuk, yuk."

I felt my senses failing and the light draining from my eyes, and then I was out.

Morning came with the singing of doves and a soft layer of dew kissing my face. I opened my eyes and found I could not move my hands. Was I tied to another stake? No, in fact, I couldn't move anything, not a toe. The realization came quickly, but with disbelief: I was buried up to my neck in god's earth, my poor head the only piece of me showing for the world to see. A glance to my left was excruciatingly ludicrous as I collected the sight of my horse suffering from a similar implantation. I did one of them double takes that was all the rage in the back east high society. My horse wouldn't out and out return my gaze, though he kept cutting angry glances at me sideways.

"I'm awful sorry," I said to my animal. I tried to imagine how much the beast must have hated me. First I made him into a gelding, and now this.

"Hey!" I called out, but as I suspected, the greasy stinkers were gone. Damn if this frontier weren't just lousy with comedians.

It was easy to picture the god-awful events which could befall an individual in my particular predicament, like wolves eating my head off or birds feeding on my eyes. There weren't nothing else to do. But I was no longer scared. Frustrated, yes. Scared?

I'd never considered how much a cowboy used his hands just casually. Without being able to scratch my ass or dig in my ear with a pinky, I was starting to lose my sense of identity. Talking was going to have to keep me entertained and awake so I could shout at any critter wandering too close.

"You know, you're a pretty good horse," I said. He looked away. "You ain't the fastest thing on four legs, but you don't fall down and you don't kick. You ain't too bad to look at neither, for a horse. Course you ain't worth a damn as far as conversation is concerned. Nice weather. I'm sorry as can be about whackin' off your pair but believe me, I saved you a ton of trouble long term. You know, my birthday is next month. You don't have to get me nothing. Card would be nice. Are your shoes comfortable?"

"They'll do."

I reckoned the weight and pressure of the earth against my body was causing a mild delirium. "I always imagined your voice differently."

"Don't say."

"Well, yeah, I do say. I thought it would be higher."

"And all this time I thought you didn't even know I existed."

A foot stirred dust by my head. "Who's there?" I asked. "Somebody here with me?"

Two booted feet stepped in front of my face, then moved back to show me legs and the upward view of the rest of a grizzled old-timer.

"What's the idear?" I said. "Sneakin' up on a fella what's buried to his neck."

"I thought you was talkin' to me," he said. He looked at my horse and slapped the side of his head. "Oh, I get it. You was talkin' to your horse and when you asked about the shoes, I thought you was askin' me and when I answered, you thought it was the horse talkin' and oh, I get it." He nodded his head happily. "My name is Epiphany Jones."

"Curt Marder."

"Pleased to meet you."

"Likewise. More so."

He looked at my head and then around the area. "Tell me, shorty, how you come to be out here like this?"

"It ain't by choice," I told him.

"Seems right." He tried to spit tobacco juice but made a mess in his beard and down the front of his shirt. "You from around here?"

"No, sir, I ain't. I was camped here real peaceful, just mindin' my own mindin's when these men—these greasy men what smelled like cat shit on a hot day, I mean I can't begin to describe how foul they smelled, and ugly, they could unnerve a buzzard, the devil hisself ain't near as ugly."

"You invite 'em?" he asked.

"Hell, no, I didn't invite 'em. What kind of fool you take me for? They showed up out of nowhere and disarmed me

110

and made me dig two big ol' holes." I shook my head, all I could shake.

"Why?"

"Why what?"

"Why'd they make you dig the holes?" he asked.

"You're lookin' at why. So they could fill 'em in around me and my horse."

"Nice looking animal."

"Thank you."

"Puttin' you in that hole seems like a heap of trouble. Why didn't they just shoot you and take your horse?"

"I didn't say they was smart," I said. "In fact, if you was to put all three of their brains on a flea's butt, he wouldn't notice." I rolled my head, trying to loosen my neck. "You gonna dig me out?"

"Wait, I think I get it. You don't want to be buried up to your neck. Let me see if'n I got this straight. You was here in your campsite, and these three men, ugly men, ugly, stinky, stupid men come uninvited and forced you to dig two holes, and then they put you in one and your horse in the other and filled the dirt in around you. I get it." He nodded.

"You gonna help me?"

"These fellas say anything during all this fuss?"

"All they said was, 'Yuk, yuk, yuk.'"

He tried to spit again, then stood and stretched his back. "Like them coolies on the railroad says, 'Sooo solly.'"

"What?"

"Cain't help you."

"Why not?"

"A pappy cain't go round underminin' the doin's of his boys. Ain't right." He shook his head. "Ain't right. You're

111

in a mess. Any fool can see that and I might have been willin' to bend the rules to help you out, but after the way you talked about my sons . . . why, those boys are like kin to me. You seem like a white enough fella, but I just cain't see helpin' you after all you done said."

"Would it help if'n I apologized?"

"We could try it," he said.

"I'm sorry."

He closed his eyes for a spell, then looked at me. "Nope, didn't do a damn thing for me." He started away. "Take care, shorty."

14

A MAN PLANTED UP to his Adam's apple in God's good earth is certainly a pitiful sight, and I'm sure you can imagine that a man suffering such a condition might easily become bitter. I didn't hold no grudges against the Yuk Yuk brothers—they was just doing what the good Lord intended for scum-sucking, lily-livered bumps on horse biscuits to do. It was their natural job. And besides, I was scared of them. Don't make no sense to hold no grudge against somebody dangerous. But Bubba, that conniving darkie, now he was to blame. Why was it he who rode off across that river instead of me? Why did I have to scour the more deadly territory in which was hiding the stinky siblings?

When a man is separated from his whole body, he has an impulse to reflect. I had always resisted such impulses in the past, having found the results somewhat untidy, frequently shameful and certainly fruitless. And reflecting was an embarrassing activity for a man to admit to. I remember meeting this poet fellow just before I deserted the army at Bull Run. He was sitting under a tree, and I asked him what he was doing.

He said, "Young man, I'm reflecting."

I studied him for a spell.

Then he said something about his body being a temple. His eyes was glazed-like and he spit when he talked. His long hair was dirty, and he scratched his beard a lot. He looked at the sky and said, " 'I celebrate myself, and sing myself.' I wrote that. Seems so long ago now."

"I cain't sing a lick," I told him.

He nodded and asked me a funny question. "How much do you suppose you weigh?"

But reflect I did. I thought about Sadie first and about how she had only one dress to wear and about how I made her chop the wood in the rain. Then I thought about cows I had milked and Mormons I had seen on the road once and horses I had broke and money loaned to me that would never get paid back. I wondered where my hat was and if Adam and Eve had belly buttons and I tried to recall the words to "Rock of Ages."

On my way west, I had met a man dressed in black with a preacher's collar who told me he was one of them Catholic priests. He crossed himself a lot and told me the story of Job while we sat in a saloon in Lawrence, Kansas. It was a rowdy place full of drovers and bar gals in red dresses. We had to shout at each other to converse and he wouldn't hear of me getting up and leaving.

" 'And the Lord said unto Satan, Whence comest thou? Then Satan answered the Lord, and said, From going to and fro in the earth, and from walking up and down in it,' " was how he started and let into the tale.

I could not believe what poor Job had to suffer through. It was dang awful. Losing everything and hurting all the time and others grinding with his woman. "How," I said finally, "could God do such things to a decent white fella like Job?"

The priest told me the rest of the story, then nodded his head. "Curse God, and die," he boomed above the sound of the piano and a woman beginning to sing.

"How did Job take it?" I shouted, watching the painted woman giving forth the song.

"Faith, my son," he said. " 'The price of rubies is above wisdom.' " He paused. "I think I got that backwards. Hmmm, I'll have to look it up."

"Still. I mean somebody should have at least told him they was sorry. Didn't the Lord even split what he got from the bet with him?"

" 'Let me be weighed in an even balance that God may know my integrity.' Job, chapter thirty-one, verse six." Then he gave me a long look. "How much do you think you weigh?"

Time became meaningless. I felt right funny having that thought. But shadows of passing clouds and birds and sleep and the coming of night and day all run together something fierce. I found myself wishing I could sing.

I regained a measure of clear-headedness and looked around once more. I swear it just plain wasn't funny. I had a reckless itch scurrying all over my body in close pursuit of an aggravating tickle. I tried to quit thinking about either by talking again. Whatever day it was, it was wearing on and thin, and by the afternoon I was clean out of conversation and got the impression my horse weren't listening no way. I took to whistling, but that can dry a man's mouth out in pretty short time.

Then there was another pair of feet staring me in the face. I couldn't suppress a crazed giggle. The angle was, of course, different, but I knew right off it was the little

115

potion vendor with the loose cards who Wide Clyde McBride tried to kill.

"Hey, I know you," I said.

"You do? I can't say the same."

"Well, there's more to me than meets the eye."

He chuckled, his shoulders shaking in fast up-and-down jerks. "I suppose that's true. Are you aware you're buried up to your neck?"

"If you'd gived me another minute I'da come to it on my own." I studied his lace-up shoes. "Don't you remember me? I saved your life."

"I believe I'd recall a man who performed such a marked service, but I can't place your face. Are you tall?"

"Not so's you'd notice," I said.

"Are you fat?"

"Nope."

Do you limp?"

"Nope."

"Then I can't say there's any feature to your person that might distinguish you from any other filthy cowpoke I have come across in these parts."

"You was in a saloon and Wide Clyde McBride—you might not know him by name—now, he's *fat*, big as a pig barn and twice as smelly—well, he and a couple other fellas caught you with a stray ace and took to beatin' on you. I drew their attention and out you scooted into the street away to safety. You got any water?"

He pulled a flask from his pocket and knelt down. He gave me a stingy sip and stood up again. "I remember that, I do. You were gagging on something, right?"

"That was me. It was my gaggin' what saved you from being beat dead into the floor."

116

"Maybe."

"How do you figger maybe?"

He scratched his chin. "I could have probably handled the lot of them."

"You've got a bad drinkin' problem. What's your name again? Greengrocer?"

"My name is Greenfeld."

"Greenfeld," I repeated. "Tell me, what kind of name is that?"

"Jewish."

"Jewish? You mean you're a Jew?"

"That's what I mean."

I blew out a breath. "Don't that beat all." I looked at him. "Turn around."

"What?"

"Turn around. I want to get a good look at you. I ain't never seen no Jew before. Come on, just twirl around once so I can see."

He did.

"You ain't no such thing," I said.

"What are you talking about?"

"You ain't no Jew no more than I'm an Injun."

"Listen, Cochise." He dropped to a knee and looked at my face. "I am a Jew."

"Where are your horns then?"

"Christ."

"See, see what you said! What kinda Jew goes around sayin' that? I heard Jews had horns on their heads, but your head's just like mine."

"Hardly."

"Hey, how about diggin' me outa here. I mean, I did save your life and all that."

"I'd like to thank you for that bit of western heroism, but I'm afraid I can't help you." He stood up.

"Why the Sam Hill hell not?"

"Got to go back along the trail and find my horns. I didn't know they were missing."

"Lordy Christmas, man. Don't be so dang sensitive. They was right about that, though—you Jews is awful touchy."

"I think I know how you got yourself into that hole." he said.

"Yeah? How?"

"Talking."

"Shows how much you know."

The little man stepped away. Ill-mannered son of a mudrat. They was right about that too.

Damn if time didn't just wiggle like a worm in my brain and I looked up and found an Injun staring down at me. I weren't sure at first if he was real, but his horse's front hoof kicking up dust told me he was. He weren't wearing no paint; however, he did hold a rifle by his side. I glanced around as far as I could, trying to determine if he was all by his lonesome. He looked at me for a long while, maybe trying to decide if I was real. Finally, I just had to say something.

"Shoot me or piss on me, but do something, you red bastard."

What I said didn't stir him none. Then, like a flash of hot lightning he was on his knees by my naked head with his knife drawn. I lowered my chin to offer token resistance to the slitting of my throat. But he didn't slice my apple. He started to dig. I was astounded. The heathen was

118

rescuing me, saving my life. I thought for a second that maybe he was just digging down to my pockets. He dug and dug. I thought, what if he only digs me out to my elbows — these heathens was cursed with a sick sense of humor. I quelled any expressions of jubilation or gratitude.

Damn if he didn't dig me clear right down to my waist so that my hands was free. I worked my fingers slowly. They felt like rigy-morti had settled in. Breathing was a far sight easier. He stopped digging and stabbed the blade down in front of me. I looked at him. He stood and turned away.

"Hey," I said, "I'm too weak to dig."

He didn't say nothing, just walked to his horse, where he drank from a skin bag. He offered some water to his animal in a cupped hand. He then tossed the vessel to me. I drank it all, my dry mouth working like a sponge. He said something about drinking it slow, his first words to me, but I didn't listen. I should have heeded his warning, because my belly twisted into a knot and I gave back nearly as much as I swallowed.

It was clear that he was done with digging, but he didn't seem in no hurry to leave me there. He sat on a stump and watched my progress. Dusk was coming on, and the work was making me somewhat less silly. Was the Injun letting me dig myself free just so he could shoot me with his rifle? What was brewing in his evil, twisted mind? He built a fire that glowed smartly in the dark.

Finally, I was free. My legs cracked as I reminded them of bending, and I rubbed my body to get the blood moving and to renew feeling. Still, the Injun only sat there.

"You got a name?" I asked.

He pointed to the knife in my hand.

"What?"

He pointed to my horse. I rubbed my aching elbows. I was ready to let the horse stay there.

He lifted his rifle and leveled the barrel at me.

"Awright," I said. "You could at least tell me your name."

It took me the rest of the night to dig the beast clear. The Injun held the rifle on me the whole while. My horse stumbled around a bit in the early morning, then found his legs. The rising sun was behind the Injun, making him a silhouette so I couldn't see his face. He mounted and stepped away.

I tried to climb on my horse's bare back, but he was having none of it. So, I walked, leading the animal and following the red man.

15

ON LEGS LIMPER THAN a milked cow's teats, I traced the
path of the heathen for several hours. At least, it seemed
that long, my being hard-pressed to sight any landmarks
in the distance as we traveled. I observed only the dust in
the wake of the Injun's horse. Nor had I noted the position
of the sun when we started out. In fact, I had no idea why
I was following the man at all. But I was.

We came to the crest of a hill and when I could see over
to the other side, my heart went all aflutter. A whole regi-
ment of blue-clad United States of America cavalry was
out there on the flat, parked there like they'd been there
forever. Tents was everywhere, and the air smelled of
beans and gunpowder. Soldiers drilled on either side of the
camp, the barrels of their rifles gleaming in the midday sun.
We climbed down the hill, and the Injun wandered toward them as casual as any white man. He was even greet-
ed like a friend by several of the soldiers.

I was stopped by a sentry. "What is your business here?"
a fat blue private asked me.

"Business?" I muttered to myself. "You see, I was
robbed—" I stopped, thinking better of detailing my abuse.
"And I was left for dead. But your Injun friend there came

along and I followed him here so he wouldn't get lost. I need food and water." My horse gave me a nudge with his snoot. "And water for my ride."

"Who was it robbed you?" the private asked.

"Injuns. Big'uns. Mean'uns."

He regarded me for a long second. "Okay," he said. "Go on over to that tent and tell it to the quartermaster." He pointed. "Tell him what you told me and maybe he'll fix you up." As I started away he said, "How'd you figger on keeping the Injun from gettin' lost if you was followin' him?"

I shrugged and walked on.

There was armed white men everywhere, as far as my eyes could see. At first I felt safe as a babe in his mama's lap, but then I began to worry that somehow they'd know I was a deserter and string me up.

I got to the quartermaster's tent and stepped inside. The fella was itty bitty, and he gave me a hard look right off like I'd said something about his size. Then he looked past me out the flaps of the tent and back to me.

"Well?" he said.

"I was robbed on the road by big Injuns who left me for dead and I followed your Injun traitor to the camp and the private outside said that maybe you could help me. Maybe."

"What do you want from me?"

"Food," I said. "A couple blankets. They stole my saddle."

He grimaced a bit and sucked his teeth. Then he reached to the pile of blankets behind him and peeled off two, tossed them into my chest. "You eat when everybody else eats."

I turned to walk out and stopped. "This don't mean I'm in the army, do it?"

"No, it don't mean you're in the army."

I took the blankets outside and set them down by a hanging water bag. I drank some and put down a bucket for my horse. Glancing around I spied the Injun what dug me free, standing and talking with a couple of soldiers. He pointed in my direction and the others wagged their fingers at me like they wanted to know if they was looking at the right fella and then they all laughed, a big belly laugh that set me low and made me consider my odor.

"What's your name, civilian?" This from a man who sneaked up behind me and gave me a start. "Easy, fella, I didn't mean to undo your colon."

I observed his narrow, mustached face. "My name is Marder," I told him.

"Staff Sergeant Ridley Phardt. You can call me Rip, though. Everybody calls me Rip, 'ceptin' my ma, who calls me Riddle—well, used to call me that before she died. I asked why she called me Riddle once and she just laughed. But you can call me Rip."

"Awright, Rip. I'm Curt." I looked around. "I sure was surprised to find you boys here. I run onto some tough luck. Got robbed and made awful fun of by some stinkin' illiterate bastards."

"Be careful what you say now," Rip said, shaking his head. "Most of my family is practicing illiterates."

"Sorry."

"They're gettin' right good at it."

"Well, these boys had it down pat."

"Where you from?" he asked.

"I got me a little spread east and south of here, near the town of ——. Had a place."

"What you doin' out here?"

"Lookin' for the bushwhacking snake pimples what attacked my home, burned it to the ground, killed my stock and stole my woman. I'm out here trackin' 'em down so's I can get my Sadie back and see that justice is done." A tear dotted the corner of my eye.

"Buck up, partner. So, you're a tracker?" he asked.

"I'm the best tracker in these parts. I once tracked a crow for six miles in a dust storm."

"Wow, that's good."

"Thanks."

He sniffed a little. "Did you know you stink somethin' fierce?" he asked.

"The notion occurred to me."

"You know, a tracker with your talents can make a pretty penny with the army."

"I ain't joinin' nobody's army."

"That's what great about it. A tracker ain't got to join up. He just gets paid." He smiled. "I'll take you to the colonel."

"How about that?"

"But you cain't be goin' there smellin' like you do. You gotta get cleaned up. I mean you smell worse than a skunk what's done died of disease and got maggots just eatin' away at his innards."

"Okay, okay."

"I'll take you to the creek. You can use my soap."

At the creek I scraped off my clothes and slipped into the icy water. I lathered up and thought about washing my clothes, but that was such a bother. Rip sat on the bank and watched me the whole while. He started talking.

"You hear the one about the two Injuns who go into a saloon in Virginia City? Well, the bartender says, 'We don't serve Injuns in here.' And one of the Injuns says—" He stopped and looked at the grass in front of him. "What does that Injun say? I cain't remember, but ain't that almost funny? I heard it told with niggers too and it's just as good. Wanna hear it?"

"Maybe later."

He took to gawking at me again.

"Your soap lathers up real nice," I said.

"Be sure to wash under yer arms," he said.

I nodded.

"And get behind them ears."

"Right."

"Kinda lather up around your thighs again."

I looked at the man. I waded out of the creek, walked to my clothes, gave them a good shaking out and put them on.

"You know, if'n you're as good a tracker as you say, you can make a killin'. The colonel wants an Injun named Big Elk real bad."

"Big Elk?"

"Yeah."

"Hell, I can find Big Elk for him," I said. "I know where he is right now."

He stopped cold and stared at me.

I hadn't known that Big Elk was such a big deal. Rip couldn't shut up all the way to the colonel's tent.

"Oh yeah, the colonel really wants that red dog. He

killed five whites who were trying to steal some horses from him. And he shot at a couple of white preachers who was trying to enlighten his people with a little whiskey."

"What's this territory comin' to?"

"He's a bad one."

If I had known all this about Big Elk, I woulda been more scared and a sight more respectable. I was thankful with renewed gusto for having been set free from the stake short of cooking till done.

The colonel's tent was in the middle of the camp and was made obvious by its size and the two large flags flying at either side of the entrance, a United States and a Seventh Cavalry.

"Sergeant Rip Phardt to see the colonel," Rip said to the young lieutenant seated at a small desk just outside the flaps of the tent.

"On what matter of business, Sergeant *Rip Phardt?* If that really is your name?"

"It is, and the matter is that this here stinkin' cow rat what come into camp, what I done tried to get cleaned up and presentable, claims to be a tracker of notable repacities."

"Oh yeah?" The officer looked at me.

"Says he knows where Big Elk is hid out," Rip said.

"I've seen his camp," I said.

"Colonel," the lieutenant called into the tent.

A golden-locked, wild-mustached and goateed man swaggered immediately out into the light. "I heard, Knoys," he said, and he fixed his steely blue eyes on me.

I don't know why, but I snapped to attention.

"What's your name?" the Colonel asked.

"Marder."

126

"My name is Colonel George A. Custer. Perhaps you've heard of me."

I said nothing.

"George Armstrong Custer."

"No, sir."

"Drat," he said under his breath. Then to Rip, "Good work, Sergeant. Dismissed."

Rip saluted and tore himself away.

"Come on in here, Marder. Lieutenant, bring us some food." To me, "You are hungry?"

"Yes, sir."

The inside of the tent was somethin' else altogether. It was decorated up like a whorehouse. There was rugs on the dirt floor and a couple of tables and a desk and a little table with a checkerboard painted on top with them chess fellas on it. A painting of the colonel rested on an easel behind the desk, showing that same steel-blue stare I seen outside. The colonel paced, twirling his mustache with the thumb and forefinger of his left hand and palming the handle of his sword with his right hand.

"I suppose you're all too familiar with the heinous activities of one Big Elk," Custer said. "That Indian's scalp will be the crowning feather in my cap. The heathen has no respect for the ownership of land. I mean, we take it and they want it back, keep coming back. Hunting lands, they say. Fishing waters, they say. That's not it, though. I know why. I know why."

"Why? Why?"

"Sit down," Custer said and pointed to one of the chairs at the little table. "I'll tell you why. To confuse me. To confuse *us*. To make us question ourselves, our values. We *must* have more land than we need. It's essential to our maintaining a balance between greed and hypocrisy, between unhealthy subsistence and needless, uncontrolled growth. 'Be assured, my young friend, that there is a great deal of *ruin* in a nation.' It's the American way. I'm talking about our way of life, man. And they're trying to take it away from us. From *me*. First the slaves wanting to be free and now these red heathens. It's enough to make you spit in bath water."

"I often have," I said.

He sat down suddenly in the chair opposite me, so quickly that he gave me a start. "President Lincoln and I once chatted briefly at a party. Some kind of thing. A most unsightly man. He didn't have any teeth back here." He pointed back into his mouth. "He never would have made it through West Point."

A private brought in a tray of bread and raw meat.

"Set it down anywhere," Custer said. The private set it on the corner of the table between us. Custer waved the man away without looking at him. "He said to me that he just hated signing that Emasculation Proclamation, but he had to. That war wasn't about slavery. That war was about the American Way. Just what I've been talking about. As my father put it, 'To die with your hand in another man's pocket is no sin, but to die sitting down . . . well, that's a horse of another feather.' "

My eyes were fixed on the food and I was frowning. "What is it?"

"That meat is raw," I said.

"Of course it is. A *man* eats his meat raw. Go ahead and have at. It'll make your balls bigger than apples. I eat raw meat all day long, every day. You should see my balls. They're something to behold. You play chess?"

128

I took a couple of pieces of bread as he removed the tray from the board and set it on the floor by his feet.

"Don't know how," I said.

"I'll teach you. The movement of the pieces is quite simple. Like most of the singular actions of battle. But it's how you put it all together that's special. It's a warrior's game, a king's game. This piece is called a pawn." He held it up in front of my face.

I nodded.

"Say it."

"Pawn."

"Good." Another. "Knight." He prompted me with a nod of his head.

"Knight."

And so it went. Then he showed how they all moved. I was dizzy with hunger. I heard the dinner bell outside.

"They cook their meat," he said.

"Wimps," I said.

"Let's start. I'll be white. White always moves first."

I didn't have no idea what was going on, but every time I looked at the board, Custer had put a piece right in a place where he taught me I could take it. He had pieces flying everywhere and I just killed them. He would mutter "Drat" each time.

"We're here to get Big Elk and then it's back to fighting those damn Sioux. I've been having fun in that war." He took a bite of meat. "So, you've seen Big Elk's camp."

"Yes, sir."

"Well, where is it? Can you take me there?"

"I can tell you where it is."

"Okay."

"Will I get paid?"

"How's a hundred dollars sound to you?"

I tried to keep my eyes from popping out of my head. "That sounds fair," I said.

"I'm going to make a name for myself out here in the west. Everybody's already forgotten that other war. Why do wars have to end?" His voice was sad. He moved his queen in front of my rook and I took her.

"Drat."

"A hundred dollars it is then." He called for the lieutenant. "Make out a voucher for Marder here for the sum of one hundred dollars."

The young officer gave me a look and went to take a seat behind the desk, took a book from the drawer.

"Where is he?" Custer asked.

"He's west of Cahoots and a little north. In the foothills, right on the river."

He put his hands up like he was praying and clapped them. "Goody."

The lieutenant came over and handed me a piece of paper.

"What's this?" I asked.

"It's a United States Government voucher," the lieutenant said. "You can cash it in at any bank in the whole country."

"I walk into a bank and give 'em this piece of paper and they give me a hundred dollars?"

"That's right."

Custer looked at the chess board. "Lieutenant, get this man out of here. No civilians in camp."

16

SOME FACTS ARE A far sight larger than others. For example, I had been able to overlook completely that I no
longer owned the land with which I was to pay Bubba. A
slightly bigger fact was that the poop hounds still had my
Sadie; this came to me like a pinched nerve in my back—I
could move so it would hurt. But the large fact in front of
me right then was that I was rich. And so, I had plans to
make. How and where was I going to spend all my money?
I sat and pondered that at the edge of the creek, my eye
peeled for Staff Sergeant Rip Phardt. Night was on good,
and I sat on one of my blankets while the other kept me
warm. I chomped on the stale bread I had been able to lift
from the tray in Custer's tent.

Sitting there, the night all still like it was, I recalled the
face of a man I saw dying in a cattle camp once. He was
wasting away with typhoid in the back of a wagon and
everybody was giving him wide berth. No one tended to
him because there was nothing to do. I looked over the
edge of the wagon at his face and asked him what he wanted. He glared at me and said, "I want to be well or dead."

"I wish I could help you," I told him.

He looked at me for a long spell, started to speak a couple of times but sucked it. Then after a long pause and a big sigh, he said, "Shut up."

I never forgot that. Not that it meant much to me. And I'll be damned if I know why it came to mind.

I decided to think about Loretta back there in Cahoots. I had money now and I would finally have her. There was a bank in Cahoots where I could cash in and, kiss heaven, two saloons full of whiskey and rowdiness.

Listening to the trickling creek water, I had a weird feeling. There was something about telling Custer of Big Elk's whereabouts that didn't set right with me. The notion was malignant, and soon it was burning a hole in the top of my head. A case of conscience is a needling and exceedingly useless condition. I told myself that all them people was just Injuns and I felt better.

I folded the voucher and stuffed it into my breast pocket. My horse blew out a snort behind me and I gave a glance his way. I laid down with a log as a pillow.

In the morning it dawned on me. I didn't know where I was. I drank some water from the creek, then dipped my face in to get good and awake. I stood and walked back to the camp's edge and stopped a sentry.

"Where are we?" I asked.

"Well, we're right here," he said.

"No, I mean, where is here?"

"Well, I reckon, that's where we is."

I looked at him.

"The camp's behind me," he said.

"How do I get to Cahoots?" I asked.

"Oh," he said and smiled new understanding. "Well, you see, you follow this here crick south until you come to a bigger crick and then you follow it south till you come to an even bigger crick what's actually a river, and then you follow that south and you'll come to the road that'll take you east to Cahoots."

"Thank you," I said. "That was right clear."

"Clear?"

"Your directions. They was good."

"Thank you," he said.

"You're welcome."

I backed up a few steps, then turned and walked quickly, knowing where I was going but awful foggy about where I'd been. Before I was too many yards away I realized that I was setting off into the wilds without a gun. I went back into the camp to find Rip.

I found him finishing up a mess of eggs and bacon. I looked over to see the cook cleaning up.

"I need a gun," I said.

"I believe I can scrounge one up for your empty *holster*."

I'll hurry through this part here. Weren't much to it. He just thought I should have another bath before setting out on the trail.

I had the gun and I was the cleanest man in the filthiest clothes in the territory.

I felt a heap better with a gun fastened to my side. I followed the creek and soon I was deep in the middle of the wild nowhere. As I came down from the high country, the land got dry and the trees disappeared and the creek shrank. There weren't nothing to look at. It was a painful stroll through chloroform, but I had to keep going. Any

133

pause at all would have been fatal for sure, as I would have given in to fatigue and weakness from hunger. But like any real man of the frontier, sheer stupidity saw me through as I concentrated on the singular task of sticking to my horse's back.

At last I found the road to Cahoots. The wagon-rutted lane was drier than a desert beetle's cough. I was relieved to be on the right trail, yet filled with a fresh spirit of fear as I observed evidence of my fellow beings. The voucher suddenly became heavy and made my pocket sag. I worked at appearing destitute. I must have been giving a fairly adequate performance, because I rode down the main street of town without drawing a single glance.

The afternoon was hotter than sin, and it occurred to me to go buy a bath just to cool off some, but I didn't have any money yet. I eyed the bank, which would be closed till morning, then hitched my horse in front of the Silver Dollar, where I hoped to find Loretta. Even though it was early, there was plenty of drunken men and gals all done up in paint and ruffly dresses. Loretta was not in sight. I made my way through the sweaty bodies to the bottom of the stairs. The player piano kicked in and caused my heart to jump. I started up the steps and was stopped by a man of extraordinary size wearing a red vest and a string tie, and though he seemed not to be inclined toward speech, he made it clear I had gone as far as I was going.

"I'm looking for Loretta," I said.

He folded his arms and stared at me down his nose.

"I'll just be a minute. If I could just see her."

Nothing.

"Could you tell her I'm down here? Tell her a man

named Marder is here." I looked at his rock-hard puss. "No dice, eh?"

Finally a response as he shook his head.

Outside in the street I observed that my two blankets had been stolen from my horse's back, but it made no never mind, because after I cashed in my paper I'd be buying me one of them silver-studded saddles with Spanish stirrups.

I went around into the alley between the Silver Dollar and the building next to it. I couldn't find no stairs to the second floor, so I climbed some crates and pulled myself onto the roof. I worked my way around front to the windows.

I put my face to the glass and looked inside. There was a gal dressed down to her flimsies sitting on a nekked fella and she was rubbing his back. She was real pretty-like. He was real big and I got scared she might look my way and scream, so I moved on. The next window was dark, but I remembered it as the window I had used to escape Loretta the last time I seen her.

I tapped lightly on the pane and waited. I tapped again. "Loretta," my voice hardly more than a breath. "Loretta," a little louder. I stopped as a couple of cowboys walked past below, down the middle of the street. I pushed up on the sash, gave another faint call, then opened the window wider. I squeezed through clean without knocking nothing over and stood still. I was happy to be off the roof.

"Loretta."

"Who's that?"

"Loretta?"

The bed creaked and then there was somebody standing in front of me.

"Yeah, it's Loretta."

"It's me, Curt Marder." After no answer, "Dirt."

She punched me in the stomach and folded me over. Air rushed out of me.

"Shhhh," she said.

"Don't you remember me?"

"I remember you." Then she slapped my face and stood me up.

"Shhhh," I said.

"What are you doin' here?" she whispered through tight teeth. "You know who's in that bed right there?"

"No."

"That there is the toughest, meanest, most dangerous man in this whole territory. He's wanted for robbery, assault and murder. He's got knife and bullet scars everywhere on his body, and I mean everywhere. It hurts me just to think of what I seen on him. I'll have you know that downstairs he ate a whiskey glass, chewed it up and swallowed it." She was quiet for a second. "Maybe I should wake him up."

"I'd be really obliged if'n you didn't." I was shaking in my boots. "Loretta, I've got some money now is why I'm here. I've got a lot of it. Almost."

"Get out of here before I do wake him."

"Please, I'll pay double. I haven't been able to git you off my mind. Every waking moment I see your face. I think I'm in love with you. I'll pay triple."

"Okay, okay, but you got to git out of here right now. If he wakes up I'm the one who'll have to clean up the blood."

I was backing out the window as she finished. "So, I can come back?"

"Yeah. Now git."

I was on the roof again and she was to the window. "Tomorrow? I can come back tomorrow?"

She closed the window and drew the shade.

17

THE MORNING FOUND ME hunkered down in the very
hay where the dead man had lain in the livery. I left my
horse tied up to the fence at the rear of the stables. I was
starving and beside myself waiting for the bank to open.
So, I went there and stood around outside the front door.
I could see the tellers inside getting things ready at their
windows. The Cahoots Savings and Usury Bank was set
on a corner facing the clock of the town hall. I had fifteen
minutes to wait, so I slid on my butt down the wall to the
planks.

In pretty short order there were four more fellas waiting
with me and they was watching the clock too. I nodded
to one of them, and though he smiled at me, he didn't seem
none too friendly. They looked up and down the street a
lot, then at each other.

"Where's K.?" asked one.

"He'll be here," another said.

"He's always late."

"He'll be here."

The doors were unlocked and opened and I walked inside, but the other men didn't follow. I stepped up to the
first teller's window and slapped down my voucher.

"Give me my money," I said.

The teller was a weasely-looking little fella with glasses dripping down his skinny nose. He picked up the paper with the tips of his long fingers like it had been dipped in shit. "And what is this?"

"It's a United States Government voucher," I said.

"Meaning?"

"Meaning I'm cashin' it in for a hundred dollars," I said. "Just like it shows right there." I pointed to the bottom of the voucher.

"And you expect me to honor this?"

"Of course I expect you to honor it. It's honorable. I got it from the army."

"I've never seen one of these before." A finger chased his glasses back up his snoot. "Imagine you're me," he said. "And a dirty, scummy fellow like yourself comes into the bank and gives you this little piece of paper signed by a Lieutenant N. O. Knoys with no kind of stamp or nothing."

"Okay," I said. "Now imagine you're me."

"We can stop right there," he said.

"Hey, I imagined I was you," I told him.

"Well, that's one thing."

"Listen, I need that money."

"Actually, that's quite apparent." He nodded and smiled to a woman stepping up to the next teller.

"You're making trouble for yerself. I'll have you know that I'm the best tracker in the United States Army Seventh Cavalry and if'n I don't get my money, I'm gonna go back and tell my commandin' officer and he'll have you drafted."

"Mr. Prickle," the teller caught a man passing behind him.

"Yes, Fickle?" The older man stopped and put on a pair of spectacles.

"This *gentleman* here has presented me with this paper and he's requesting one-hundred dollars."

Prickle glanced over Fickle's shoulder at the voucher, then looked up at me with a sneer. "Do you have any sort of identification?"

"What?"

"Do you have anything that proves that you are who you say you are?"

"I know I'm me."

"But how am I supposed to know you're you? What if you weren't you and you came in here to me saying you were you when you really weren't you. And suppose I gave you the money and then the real you walked in and asked for your money and I couldn't give it to you because you already had it. Wouldn't that upset you?"

I tried to shake my head clear. "Well, it would be right upsettin' for one of us, but I'll take my chances."

"How would you feel if you were me?" Prickle asked.

"I cain't say. How would you feel if—"

Prickle stopped me with a raised hand.

"He tried that with me too," Fickle said.

Prickle sighed loudly and looked at Fickle. "Give him the money. Just get him out of here before the other customers notice him."

I reckon I should have taken umbrage, but I was all out. And I was giddy to get my money. I felt light as I watched Fickle count it out in paper money. I liked paper money. It weren't heavy like coins.

Just as I had taken it into my hands and begun to enjoy the feel of it, the doors of the bank were kicked open, and in came them fellas what was waiting outside, plus one extra who shouted "Imagine you're me and I don't get what I want!"

"It's the Keating gang," a trembling Fickle said, his glasses falling from his face.

Before I could stash my bills away into my britches, they was snatched from my hand and a gun barrel was stuck rudely under my nose.

"Hey, that's mine," I said.

"Imagine that."

"Okay, ladies and gentlemen," Keating said. "This is indeed a robbery, but we'll conduct it like business. I want you to know that it ain't nothing personal. I like your money. My boys here like your money. You probably like your money, too, but then I don't know you." He smiled wide. "It's a shame we can't all like it together. Get it, every last dime, boys."

The robbers jumped the counter and entered the vault and cleaned out every cent. I swallowed hard and, doing so, happened to look down and saw on the floor a twenty dollar gold coin which got loose. I placed my foot over it.

After his men had filed out, Keating himself paused at the door. "It's been a pleasure doing business with you, friends."

I bent down like I had a pain in my belly and collected the twenty dollar piece off the floor. I palmed it and held it against my leg.

Fickle observed me as I stood straight.

"That was scary," I said.

He just stared.

I spied my voucher on the counter in front of the teller. I reached for it, but he grabbed it away from me and stuffed it into his drawer.

"That's mine," I said.

"Not anymore. It's the bank's."

"I didn't sign nothing."

"You were not required to sign anything." He grinned at me. "Did you pick something up off that floor?"

"Pardon?"

"I believe I witnessed you picking something up from that floor, the bank's floor. I know I saw you do that. Now, why don't you hand it over."

"It's mine," I said.

"No, I'm afraid it's not. Your money was paper. That there is a coin."

I started to back away toward the door. "Money is money," I said.

"Mr. Prickle," Fickle called. "Mr. Prickle, would you please come here?"

I turned and ran out of there as fast as I could.

"Stop, thief!" I heard.

My heart was working extra hard, and I tried to slow my legs to a walk on the street so I wouldn't attract attention. I looked at the coin in my hand and saw a meal and a whiskey and a hour with Loretta.

I slipped into the Silver Dollar and parked my butt at a table. I asked for a whiskey and a plate of eggs and beans. The place was empty except for a poker game in the corner that was an obvious carry over from the previous night. I finished eating, paid and walked up the stairs, my pocket jingling with change. I could already smell Loretta's perfume. I stood just outside her door and breathed deeply. I knocked.

The door opened a crack. "Oh, it's you," Loretta said.

"That's right. And I've got money."

"Well, it's gonna be three dollars for you," she said.

"Three dollars?" I couldn't believe it. That was a lot of money. "That's a lot of money," I said.

"You're a special case," she said. "But if you don't want me . . . " She started to close the door.

"Wait." I looked up and down the hallway, then pulled some coins from my pocket. I gave her half. "You'll get the other half after we're done." I showed her my money, then put it back in my pocket.

Loretta opened the door and I stepped into her chamber and sucked in the sweet smells. I was naked faster than a lizard digs into the sand. I stretched out on the bed.

"You're eager," she said, slipping out of her robe. "Don't get no ideas about any rough stuff."

"Wouldn't dream of it." I watched as she slowly undressed. It was real exciting the way she pulled that nightgown over her head. I showed my approval, but she didn't seem much impressed. I guess a professional can't be running around showing emotion.

She was down to the last layer of her delicates when the door smashed open.

"That's him," Fickle said, pointing his crooked finger at me.

"You're under arrest, son," the sheriff said.

"What for?" I asked, covering my privates with the sheet.

"Bank robbery," the badged man said.

"Jesus Christ on a crutch," I said.

"And blasphemy," the sheriff said. "I also happen to be the local preacher."

I looked at the again veiled Loretta.

"Get your britches on, boy. I cain't be marchin' you down the street to the jailhouse in yer birthday suit."

I grabbed my britches and stepped into them. While doing up my buttons, I asked, "Is there anything I can say to help myself?"

"Afraid not."

"I didn't do it," I said.

"Got a witness." He threw a thumb back to indicate Fickle, who was smiling his skinny little smile. "But I myself heard the blasphemy. You're in deep pucky, cowboy. Bank robbery will get you sent to the state prison, but blasphemy—well, we hang blasphemers in these parts."

"I didn't mean to say it."

He shook his head real sad-like. "That's too bad. That means you're possessed by Satan hisself. In which case you must be hanged by the neck till clean out of life. This just ain't your day, is it?"

18

I WAS IN A pretty kettle of worms, awright. The sheriff was polite as an ugly army nurse as he ushered me down the stairs and across the saloon. I carried my boots and he carried my gun. It was difficult to believe I was the same fella what rode into town without attracting even a sideways glance from a stray pup. Now, everybody was gawking and pointing and making comments. If I hadn't been caught up with the notion of hanging I might have been embarrassed.

When we got to the jailhouse, the sheriff, whose name it turned out was Burp, got a little rougher. He pushed me down into a chair by his desk and slapped me across the top of the head.

"Want some hot chocolate?" he asked.

"No sir."

"I know what you're thinkin'," he said as he sat. "You're thinkin' that Burp's a funny name."

"I wasn't thinkin' no such thing."

"Let me tell you, Burp's a good old western name. My older brother Wyatt did more to tame this territory than any white man."

"I've heard his name."

He nodded.

I looked at the wall behind the sheriff. It was cluttered with WANTED posters of nasty-looking fellas. One caught my eye. I recognized him as one of the men what stole my Sadie. It was the one who had her hung over his saddle. He was wanted dead or alive, and the reward was one thousand dollars. My heart stood still. And that was just for him.

"I didn't rob no bank," I said.

"Fickle, the teller, said he seen you plain as the shit on yer boots, son. You had what was left of the money in your britches. You ran out of the bank. A whole mess of folks happened to see that one."

"I'm sorry about the blasphemin," I said.

"Oh, I'll let that go. I get riled right when I hear it, but it wears off pretty quick."

"What now?" I asked.

"Well, I gotta lock you up. And there you'll sit, rottin' away in that stinkin' cell until the circuit judge comes here on his rounds. Then we'll try you and send you to the state pokey, where you'll rot some more and learn to be a better, more efficient criminal."

"When does the judge come?"

"Let me see." He thought. "He was here about three weeks ago. So I reckon he's due back in three months."

"Three months?"

"At least."

The clang of that jail door closing was enough to make me cry. So I did. I sat on the metal cot that hung from the wall by chains. Then I realized I weren't alone. There was a young nigger in the cell with me.

"What you lookin' at, boy?" I asked.

He was sitting on the floor, not actually facing me. He looked down at his feet.

I heard some noise outside. I got up and walked to the barred window. I saw two men hammering on a gallows. I looked at the black boy.

"What'd you do?" I asked.

He didn't say nothing.

"I asked you a question, boy."

"I didn't do nothin'."

"Then why they got you in here?"

"They says I killed a man, but I didn't kill nobody. I ain't never even held a gun in my hand."

"If'n they said you did it, you did it," I told him.

"But I didn't." He couldn't have been more than sixteen. "That man was already dead when I got in there. I just came in and found him. He was already stiff from being dead when I come on to him."

I went back to the bunk and sat. "So, you're waitin' for the judge too."

"I ain't gonna see no judge. They says they got to hang me soon." He sniffed a bit. "I never should have gone into that livery. I never should have come into this town."

"The livery?"

"Yessuh."

"When was this?" I asked.

"About a week ago." He looked at my eyes for the first time. "You lookin' at a dead man."

The time would have been about right. He must have wandered into the livery and found the fella that Jake shot.

And they was gonna hang this boy. I considered the fact that I could save his life by telling what I knew. All I had to say was that it was Jake who shot the man. But why would I run? That's what they'd wonder. Why would I run unless I was guilty of something?

"You believe me, don't you, mister?" the boy asked.

"Don't matter none what I believe."

He put his head down on his knees again. "Lawd," he said, "I believed in you for a long time now. Please don't let these white folks kill me. I ain't done nothin'. Please, Lawd, please get me outa this here mess." He looked up as the hammering outside got louder. "What they doin' out there?"

"Nothin'," I said. "Where you come from, boy?"

"Mississippi."

"You come out here by yerself?"

He nodded. "Ain't got no family. Ain't never had no family."

"Well then, won't nobody miss you." I was trying to make him smile. "I bet you wish you never left Mississippi now."

"You is sure right."

I looked at the bars of the door.

They brung us supper that evening. I ate mine, but the boy didn't touch his. I thought to ask his name, but for some reason I didn't want to know it.

"You gonna eat your grub?" I asked.

He shook his head.

I was jarred awake from a pretty solid sleep by a big noise. The light of early morning shone beyond the bars of the window. The black boy weren't in the cell with me. I got up and went to look outside. The boy looked even younger swinging there at the end of that rope. Should have stayed in Mississippi.

Burp came late that morning and opened the door. He leaned there and looked at me sitting on my bunk.

"You can go," he said.

"You mean I'm free?"

"Free as any American."

I didn't move. I didn't stand nor reach for my boots. "How'd I come to be free?"

"Charges been dropped," the sheriff said. "I ain't surprised none. A hangin' usually puts folks in a right charitable mood. And besides, the bank got most of its money back. Don't be lookin' a gift donkey up the ass, boy."

I slipped on a boot. "I see you hung that nigger boy."

"Yep."

"He didn't have no trial," I said.

"That's true. Of course, we didn't need one. We had any number of citizens willing to testify that they seen him kill that fella."

I got the other boot on and stood. I walked out of the cell. Burp handed me my holster and gun as I passed him.

"Stay out of trouble now," he said.

I'd been released from pokeys before, but this time I didn't feel nothing special. I didn't much feel like I was free. People in the street were back to finding me invisible, and I can't say I was sad about it. I went back to the livery to get my horse. I glanced into the stable and recalled the dead man lying there.

I got my horse and rode back along the street toward the edge of town. The gallows was coming up on my left, but it was something on my right that caught my eye.

Bubba was sitting on a crate in the alley. I got off and led my horse over to him, stood in the shadows with him, looked with him at the swinging boy.

"Marder," he said.

"Hey, Bubba." I leaned against the wall. "What you doin' here?"

"Just lookin'." He sucked in a deep breath. "They murdered that boy."

"Yep."

"I heard they was goin' to do it. I reckon I got here just a little late."

I looked at him. "Too late? Too late for what? To see it?"

He glared at me. "To stop it."

"Stop it? You're sounding like a fool. How you figger you could have stopped it."

"I reckon I would have owned up to the killin' myself." He bit off a bite of chew.

"But you didn't kill that fella," I said.

"Still." He shook his head. "Look at him. He ain't nothin' but a child."

"If'n you had come to them with that story, they would-a just hung both of you," I told him.

"How you figger?"

"I just know." I didn't tell him it was what I probably would have done.

"I hope he didn't waste no time prayin'."

"What's wrong with prayin'?" I asked him.

"Nothin' for you. It's your god."

"Did you find Jake?"

He stood up. "I know where she is. I'm gonna see if she awright, then figger out what to do."

"I don't suppose we'll ever find my Sadie now," I said. "That trail is probably colder than grandma's toes."

"That might not be true. Happy Bear told me he thought he saw them men what attacked your place. We'll find 'em and then I'll have my land and I'll stay on it and anybody comes near I'll shoot 'em." He spit juice just beyond his boots.

"Awright."

"You got somethin' you want to tell me?" he asked.

"Nope. Bubba, we'd better git out of this town before somethin' else bad happens."

"I reckon you're right," Bubba said. "I reckon also that I'll let you ride down the street while I sneak out the back way."

"I'll go your way," I said.

"No, you go on. I'll meet you west of town."

I watched Bubba as he led his mule out the back of the alley. I hadn't seen him like that before.

19

BUBBA DIDN'T TELL ME how he came to know about the hanging of the nigger boy. I figgered it was one of them jungle things. He also didn't let on how he came to know that Jake was down in the farmhouse we was watching from a stand of cottonwoods.

"You sure she's in there?" I asked.

"Nope."

"Well, what now?"

He looked up at the sky, then at me. "You're gonna ride down to the front so they can see you and come out and ask you what you want. I'll sneak up to the back and look inside and see if she's awright."

"Why don't I sneak around back while you go ridin' up to the front?"

"Because they'll prob'ly shoot me before I can open my mouth."

"You've got a point." I looked at the twist of smoke from the chimney that told us somebody was there. "What do I say when he comes out? It is the preacher man down there, right?"

"I believe so."

"Won't he recognize me?" I asked.

"Prob'ly. Just tell him you want water for your horse or somethin'. Ask him which way town is."

"And you'll be peekin' through the window?"

"Yep."

"Let me ask you somethin', Bubba." I looked back at his mule and my horse behind us. "Why we doin' this? Why we goin' to all this trouble for that girl? I'm kinda glad to be rid of her."

"I'm gonna look inside," he said. "If she's okay, then we'll leave her. We just gotta be sure she's awright."

"Why?"

"Because she's a child and we're all she's got."

"What if I say I ain't helpin'?"

"Then I'd have to say I ain't gonna help you git your woman back. That's simple."

It was pretty simple. "I want your saddle," I said. "I'll help you if'n you give me your saddle."

He didn't even look back at it, not even at me, just at the house and he said, "Awright. Take it now and put it on your horse so you don't look peculiar ridin' in bareback."

As I rode toward the front of the house, I caught a glimpse of Bubba sneaking closer. It was a fleeting sight and then he was gone. The sun was massaging my neck furiously and the thought of that water was working on me.

"Yo!" I shouted. "Anybody home?" No one came out. I called again.

The door opened, and Phrensie stepped out holding a rifle. He was dressed down to his britches and a stiff white shirt buttoned to his chin.

"What do you want?" he asked.

156

"I'm in need of water," I said. "My horse, too. My horse needs some water. You gotta any water? 'Cause we really need some. Water, that is."

He moved to the front of the porch and pointed with the rifle at the well a few steps away.

I slid off my horse and led him over to the open trough.

"I know you?" Phrensie said.

I turned to him. "You look familiar to me, too. How about that, how two people with different faces can look so familiar to each other."

"You're the fella from the stagecoach. A far sight dirtier, but you're him." He didn't smile.

"You're the preacher. Right. How's that bible enterprise of yourn goin'?"

Behind Phrensie, Bubba appeared in the doorway. His eyes was hotter than an August saddle. He picked up a log from the porch and raised it as he approached the unsuspecting preacher.

"You got any of them bibles left?" I asked.

"What?"

"I find I'm in need of a copy of the Good Book. I been runnin' into more'n my fair share of ill luck. You got any left?"

He didn't believe me at all and so cocked the lever-action Winchester.

Bubba let him have it. A silly smile cracked all over Phrensie's face and he fell to his knees before slapping face down into the dust.

Bubba went back into the house and came back out with this pretty little thing in a blue dress. I looked close, and through the paint on the face I could see it was Jake.

"Howdy Christ," I said. "That there's young Jake." Then

I looked down at Phrensie. "I think you killed him, Bubba."

"He ain't dead," Bubba said. He handed the girl his kerchief. "Here, wipe that stuff off your face."

She seemed happy to oblige.

"Why'd you hit him?" I asked.

"Look at her," he said.

I did. "I like it."

"He was gonna take her to a whorehouse and sell her." Bubba shook his head. "*Sell* her, Marder."

"That's what he told me," Jake said, more of her face showing now. "He said he'd get a lot of money for a little virgin like me."

Bubba wanted to hit the preacher again but threw the log down instead.

I went ahead and drank me some water. "You shouldn't have hit him," I said.

"Why not?"

"Because you're a nigger and they're goin' to want to string you up."

"Hell, he didn't even see me."

"I reckon that's right."

"Just the same, we'd best make tracks out of here quick. I don't want him wakin' up."

"I want to find my clothes," Jake said.

"No time for that," Bubba said. "You ride with Marder. He's got a saddle."

The three of us were back together, and I thought it was a bad thing. Child or no child, Jake had turned out to be a woman and a woman ain't never nothing but trouble. Sadie weren't nothing but trouble. Loretta weren't nothing but trouble. And since the beginning, Jake, despite her littleness, was just flat out bad luck. I heard tell one time that sailors on ships wouldn't allow no women aboard. Well, I knew why now. That nigger boy wouldn't have been strung up like he was if not for Jake. If she hadn't had that fella trying to rape her, then Bubba wouldn't have beat on him, then he wouldn't have pulled his gun and Jake wouldn't have shot him dead—and there wouldn't have been no murder to pin on that boy, and I wouldn't have had to see him dangling there.

"Okay, Bubba," I said. "Where is it we're goin' to, now that we got this critter back."

"Back to Big Elk's village. We'll let them take care of the child."

"This here is a white child," I complained.

"They won't mind."

As we rode along, I recalled my lost fortune and how I'd come by it. Could the soldiers have gotten to the Injuns yet? "We hadn't oughta be goin' to that Injun camp," I said.

"Why not?" Bubba asked.

"Well, for starters, last time we was there, them Injuns tried to burn me to a crisp at the stake. I was a mite offended by that."

"They won't do it again," Bubba said.

The child was asleep and leaning her weight into my back. I tried to adjust myself and get comfortable.

Bubba spit some tobacco juice off to the side. "We'll drop off the girl and then we'll go find your woman and you'll give me my land, and that'll be that."

I wondered what was going to happen when the nigger found out that I didn't have no land to give him anymore. He'd already beat one white man and bashed another over the head with a piece of alder. I had no way of telling how desperate he was. "About that land," I said.

"What about it?"

"I ain't altogether sure it's legal for a nigger to own land."

"I can own land. Don't you worry over that notion."

"How you know you can?" I asked.

"I know. I cain't homestead, but I can own land. I'm an American, right? Much as it shames me to own up to it. And as such, I reckon I can own me a piece of land."

"Shames you?"

"Indians don't believe any man can own the land." He spit juice on the ground. "I reckon that sounds sorta right."

"You know this girl can really git heavy on a fella's back. Jake. Jake," I called to her.

"She's asleep," Bubba said.

"Why don't you take her for a while?"

"She's asleep. Let her rest. She's been through an awful lot these past days."

"*She's* been through a lot? I didn't tell you but I was buried up to my cotton-pickin' neck by these three warts off a weasel's prick. Me *and* my horse, stuck down in the dirt like some flowers a church lady planted with nothin' but our heads pokin' out."

Bubba laughed. "That's a good one, Marder. That's real funny."

"But it's true. True as that sun settin' over there." I pointed. "They made me dig both holes."

"Your horse didn't have to dig his own?" he asked.

"What I'm tellin' you is true. They left me there in the hot sun to die and git ate by buzzards."

"I'll bite. How'd you git out?"

"I was abused by a couple of fellas. One was related to

the dung bags what buried me, and the other was a cranky Jew." I looked at his face. He didn't believe me no more than he was white. "I'd be there now if'n that Injun hadn't helped me."

"An Indian helped you?"

"Yep. This Injun was a scout for the U. S. Army Seventh Cavalry and he dug me outa the ground."

Bubba stared at me wide-eyed, then furrowed his brow.

"What?" I asked.

"The army is near?"

"Yep," I said. "And they's lookin' for your buddy Big Elk. They want him in a big way."

"They won't find him. Not if'n they're tryin' to track him."

"I wouldn't bet on it," I said.

"Why do you say that?"

I cleared my throat. "Well, er, we're, er, you know, talking about the U. S. Army Seventh Cavalry. You don't expect a band of red heathens can hide from the likes of them for long, do you?"

Bubba looked ahead at the trail. "I'm gittin' me a bad feelin'." He looked behind me at Jake. "What do you reckon makes folks do like they do?"

"You askin' me?"

"Just askin'."

"Let me ask you somethin', Bubba. Would you have really got yerself hung back there to save that boy?"

"I reckon."

"Why? You didn't even know him," I said. "You didn't know him, did you?"

"I didn't know his name, but I knew him."

"You want your saddle back?" I asked.

He shook his head.

I felt Jake stirring behind me. "Thank you for savin' me," she said.

I looked to see if Bubba had heard what she said. I didn't think he had.

"Was Bubba that found you," I said.

20

WE STOPPED OFF THE trail and settled down for the night. We sat around a little fire and didn't say much. Jake looked right nice in the blue dress in the gold of the firelight. I guess I understood why it bothered Bubba so. She was just a little child out here with nobody.

"You think it's a good thing for us to be visitin' them Injuns?" I asked. "What if we's bein' watched right now and we get followed to their camp?"

"Ain't nobody followin' us," Bubba said.

"Why we gotta go there anyway?"

"They'll raise the child up and take care of her. They'll do it like she's one of them."

"Bubba, she's white."

"I do know that."

"And they's Injuns."

"Yep."

"A white child cain't be raised by no Injuns. It ain't natural. And she's a girl. It ain't right. Why there ain't no tellin' what might happen. What if she, you know, with one of them braves?"

"I ain't goin' with the Indians," Jake said. "I want to get the men who killed my ma and pa."

"I'll get 'em for you," Bubba said.

"I ain't goin' with the Indians," she said again.

"She don't even want to go," I said.

"Who's gonna raise you up?" Bubba asked her. Then he looked at me. "You gonna raise her?"

"You is," Jake said to Bubba.

Bubba studied her for a second and sucked his teeth. "I ain't got time for no snot-nosed child what already done got me almost killed. You're bad luck. You been bad luck since I met you, and you ain't never gonna be no different." Bubba had a pained expression and he looked away.

The child's eyes flooded something awful. She laid her head down on the blanket and sobbed up a ruckus.

I looked at her shakin' like an aspen leaf, then I glanced at Bubba.

The black man didn't say nothing, but he looked at me with stone eyes that were full of sadness. He stood up.

"Where you goin'?" I asked.

"Goin' to get us some food. We got us a long ride tomorrow."

When I woke up, it was early morning and there was some kind of squirrel or rodent cooking over the fire. The child was still asleep. I looked around and located Bubba, checking on his mule's hooves. He finished and came over to the fire and sat down across from me.

"Go 'head," he said. "Help yerself." He pointed to the meat, then handed me his knife.

I sawed off a chunk from the leg and bit into it. It was full of grease and gaminess, but then what ain't. "What is it?" I asked.

"Prairie dog."

"Good."

Bubba nodded.

I chewed for a while. "Bubba, what if'n we take the child to a church. I mean, I'll even take her so there won't be no questions."

"We just now took her away from a preacher."

"True enough," I said.

"Indians," he said.

"I don't know," I said. I had to steer him clear of the village for fear of what might have happened with the soldiers. For some reason I was afraid of Bubba. Well, for several reasons, not the least of which was that it was becoming clear that he weren't impressed by the color of my skin.

Then I got to thinking about that big fat reward offered for the gang that burned my spread. I could live high and mighty with that kind of money. A thousand dollars would buy me a ranch even better than that Tucker's. Ranch? Hell, I wouldn't even have to work. To tell the truth, the desire to get Sadie back weren't burning like it might have, but then it never had. Money, now, that was another story.

"You ever kill a man, Bubba?" I asked.

He looked at me for a long spell. "Nope. Wanted to plenty of times, but ain't never killed me one."

"That killing is a bad thing," I said.

"Most times."

"Ever shoot a man?"

Bubba looked at the dying fire. "Ain't never had to do that neither." He cut a piece of meat for himself. "Course, that's what we're talkin' about doin'. Shootin' and killin'. You think you got it in you?"

"Of course I do," I said. "What about you?"

"Oh yeah. I was born with it in me. I been mad for a long time. Prob'ly gonna die mad. It won't take much for me to kill." His gaze was hard and focused on the embers.

"Funny, ain't it," I said. "Here we are, two growed men and neither one of us ain't never shot or killed nobody. And that girl there has."

"And it ain't never gonna be undone," Bubba said. "She's gotta go with the Indians. Your world'll just eat her up. She's gotta go with 'em."

I looked at her. "She's gonna hate you."

Bubba nodded. "That's awright. A little hate never hurt nobody. Better she hate me alive than like me dead."

"Bubba, you know, I ain't never owned no slaves. I'm from the north." I ate a piece of meat. "They tried to arrest me back there in Cahoots. They say I robbed the bank."

"So I heard."

"You know about that?"

"I know you was in the cell with that boy, too. Leastways, I heard it was so."

"I was. He didn't say much."

"Neither did you, I reckon."

"I didn't know they was gonna hang him so quick. I didn't even know his name."

"Tater Renfro."

"What?"

"That boy's name was Tater Renfro," Bubba said.

"He was from Mississippi," I said.

166

21

BUBBA NUDGED JAKE AWAKE and we rolled up the blankets and mounted the animals. We rode north and west into the cool of the high country. Jake was behind me again.

Bubba was in the lead when he paused us with a raised hand. He leaned forward on his mule and tilted his head to listen. He stared into the woods.

"What you seein'?" I asked him.

He didn't say nothing but urged his animal slowly on. He stopped again. This time I could see, too. A line of people was walking along the ridge right above us. Bubba kicked his mule and we climbed up the slope to what turned out to be a column of Injuns. They was mostly women and on foot. The few horses carried old ones and some bloody ones.

"What's goin' on?" Bubba stopped a squaw and asked. He dismounted.

She just looked at him.

He tried again in her language. Bubba listened to her. He nodded and looked in the direction they was coming from while she talked.

"Big Elk?" Bubba said.

The woman pointed back toward the village.

Bubba came over to my horse and pulled Jake down from behind me. He led her by the hand over to the Injun woman. He talked in Injun again.

The squaw touched Jake's face. The child pulled away, then softened.

Bubba looked at the child. "I'm sorry," he said.

"No, you ain't," Jake spit at him.

The squaw turned Jake and walked her away. Bubba pulled his gun from his holster and checked the chamber for bullets.

"What?" I asked.

"Soldiers are attackin' the village," Bubba said. He climbed back on top of his mule and gave a kick.

"And?"

"Gonna go take a look," he said.

I followed him. "You ain't plannin' on shootin' at the United States Army, are you?"

"Don't know what I'm plannin' to do," he said.

"Whoa, Bubba," I said as I halted my horse.

He stopped and looked back at me.

"I think we oughta hold up right here in the woods until you cool down a bit. I don't want you doin' nothin' stupid. 'Specially while I'm with you."

He nodded, then ignored me and rode on.

Soon we could hear the sounds of gunfire. We climbed down and tied our animals to some brush. We moved closer on foot, then crawled behind a log on a hill above the village.

The braves were shootin' arrows from behind trees at the soldiers who fired from clusters on three sides of them. The camp was lousy with dead Injuns. Then the soldiers began their charge, hundreds of them shooting and swinging swords and screaming up a terrible racket. I looked over at Bubba and saw his mouth flatten into a line. His hand pulled his gun from his holster. I pulled my gun, too. He began to get up, and I used the butt of my pistol to conk the black man on the back of the head and render him unconscious.

I watched the attack. They wasn't interested in taking prisoners. They shot this way and that and blindly into tepees and they was high on the killing. I could see it in their eyes. I saw a couple of soldiers grab Happy Bear, who was already wounded, and stake him to the ground. They laughed while they stood over him, then one of them sliced open his belly. I watched his mouth open in a scream, but with all the other noise, I couldn't hear him.

Big Elk was already dead, lying in the middle of the camp. Custer came riding in, his steed lifting his forefeet high. Custer looked like a picture. He dismounted next to the body of Big Elk. He called some of his men over and instructed them to stand back and observe. He pulled out his knife, grabbed Big Elk by the hair and cut into the Injun's scalp. The soldiers let out a cheer. I looked at Bubba and he weren't stirring a bit, but I hit him again anyway. A soldier heard the thump, and I had to duck down to keep from being seen.

The soldiers took their time rooting around for trinkets and souvenirs. Then all the blue uniforms were gone, and there weren't nothing left but dead Injuns and burning tents. I waited for Bubba to come to.

It was just about high noon when Bubba came around. I was preparing myself for getting walloped. He raised up and rubbed the back of his head while he tried to focus on the scene below. He looked at it for a long time without saying nothing. He finally got up on his knees and put his gun back in his holster. Then he stood and started down the slope toward the village. I trailed after him. He stopped and turned back to me. This was it, I thought. I steeled my jaw.

"Thanks, Marder," he said. He rubbed his crown again. "That was a right decent thing to do."

"You're welcome."

Closer, all the death was worse. There was blood and the dead had faces. Bubba shook his head. "We got us a lot of digging to do."

"I didn't know Injuns got buried," I said.

The sight of Happy Bear split open like he was made me sick. I think I cried. Bubba was sure enough bawling as he walked through the scattered bodies. Then all of a sudden he wasn't crying no more. He was now standing over the bloody head of Big Elk.

"They scalped him," Bubba said.

"Custer done it," I said.

He looked at me.

"The colonel. Colonel George Armsomethin' Custer. It was him who cut off the top of Big Elk's head."

"How do you know?"

"I seen him do it."

"How you know it was him? Custer."

I swallowed. "I'm an informed citizen, that's how. If you'd read a newspaper now and again—" I stopped as Bubba weren't listening. "The soldiers let out a hip hip huzzah when Custer done it."

"How much can a man take?" Bubba asked. He ap-

170

peared to be asking Big Elk. Then he was definitely talking to Big Elk. "I'll kill this Custer for you, my friend. I'll find him and kill him for all of us."

"Have you been sniffing bull puddy?" I asked. "Maybe I hit you too hard or somethin'. Bubba, Custer is a colonel in the United States Army. Bubba, he's the commandin' officer of the Seventh Cavalry. Bubba, he's got hundreds of soldiers around him day and night. Bubba, the man has a gun *and* a sword. Bubba, he's white."

We found what blades we could and buried each and every one of them Indians. The holes were shallow, but they got covered up. It was well into the night, in fact nearing dawn, when we was done. Bubba and I stood there, somehow without falling over, and surveyed the new cemetery.

"Damn shame," I said.

"It ain't no such thin'," Bubba said. "It ain't nothin' but the way it is." Bubba looked at the sky and I thought he was going to pray or something. He said, "Right?"

"What's that supposed to mean?" I asked. "You cain't be talkin' to the Al-big-mighty like that. You don't know what'll happen."

Bubba looked around. "Yes, I do. What kinda blind fool don't know?"

"I don't mind tellin' you, I am sick of diggin' holes in the ground."

"That's awright for you."

22

BUBBA SAID HE HAD a little money left and agreed we needed to part with it so we could eat and continue on. We rode to a tiny trading post, which was also a pony express station, called Limbo's Junction. It was out on the flat without a single bush in sight to slow down the wind tearing across the terrain like it was mad. Bubba held his hat to his head as he pushed into the store in front of me. A man who looked a year older than God come up to us, his clothes dusty brown like the country and every hair on his head and face was gray as a squirrel. He wore a wide, toothless grin.

"Windy, ain't it," he said. "I'm Limbo." He shook Bubba's hand without pause or measured glance, then mine.

"Call me Bubba," the black man said.

I told him my name.

Limbo looked out the window at the prairie. "Sure is windy. But then, it's always windy. If it ain't blowin' from this way, it's blowin' from that way. I seen me many a backward-walkin' cow out on that prairie. I seen a hawk once fly in one spot for an hour till it just died of humiliation."

Bubba looked at the skinny stock on the shelves. "We gonna need us a few supplies," he said. "Beans."

"Got beans," Limbo said.

"Shells and tobacco."

"Got all that." Limbo walked behind the counter, reached below it and came up with a jar of rock candy. "I got this too. Help yerself. On the house."

Bubba shook his head. "Thanks."

"I saw you ridin' up and I thought you might be Indians." He leaned forward and said in a quieter voice, "I trade with the Indians."

"Won't be tradin' with 'em no more," Bubba said.

"Do tell."

"Soldiers killed 'em, killed almost all of 'em."

Limbo whistled. "I like them Indians. They ain't never tried to cheat me. Not once. The soldiers try to skin me all the time." He stopped and closed his eyes. "Listen," he said. He went to the window. "Here they come."

I went to the window and looked out myself. Two riders were about a hundred yards off, dressed in army blue. "Soldiers," I said to Bubba. "Two of 'em."

"Don't matter none to us," Bubba said.

"How'd you hear 'em?" I asked Limbo.

"Yer ears git right good out here with nobody to yak to. Ain't nothing to listen to but the wind, and the wind carries things. The wind can carry things for miles and miles. Why, sometimes at night I can hear cougars snorin' in the mountains or an Indian baby cryin' 'cause it wants its mama's milk."

"I'm gonna need some coffee too," Bubba said.

"Ain't got no coffee." Limbo put the candy back under the counter.

174

The door blew open and the soldiers noised their way inside, coughing dust and swearing about the wind. Bubba moved over to the woodstove to warm his hands. He looked at me, so I walked over to stand near him. The soldiers glanced at us but made a point of showing no interest.

"Hey there, Limboy," one soldier said. He was a right big one with a wild red mustache.

The smaller one laughed. "What you been doin' out here? Been listenin' to the wind? Did you hear any screamin' and cryin'?"

"Screamin'?" Limbo asked.

"Yeah," the big one said. "Didn't you hear no screamin'? I woulda thunk sure the wind woulda carried all that noise. We killed us a tribe."

The smaller laughed like a rat and said, "Killed us a whole tribe. Big Elk and his clan – dead as the day they was born. It was somethin' to see."

The big one walked behind the counter and found the jar of candy underneath. He tossed a piece into his mouth and pushed the open jar over to his buddy. "Colonel Custer scalped that son of a bitch good." He pulled up his own hair to demonstrate. "Started here and cut him all the way around. Nice, clean, professional job."

I glanced at Bubba's face, but he weren't showing nothing. He thumbed absently through a stack of Injun blankets.

"And they couldn't fight for shit," the little one said.

"It's hard to fight when yer runnin'," the big one laughed.

The short soldier found me with his beady little eyes

what was too close to his face. "Hey, don't I know you from somewhere else?"

I shook my head.

"Sure, I seen you before."

"Afraid not," I said.

He turned his attention away from me and talked to Limbo. "Yeah, after all that killin', our boys are havin' a holiday in Cahoots." He leaned toward the old man. "But we thought we'd come out here and see if'n you got anythin' for us."

Limbo started to shake. "So, you got them Indians good, eh?"

The big one stretched. "Sweet little squaws out there, Limboy. Yeah, we give it to them heathens *real* good." Then he looked at Bubba. "Hey, nigger."

Bubba turned his eyes to the man.

"What do you think about what we been sayin'?" the big soldier asked.

Bubba shrugged. "Don't know."

"Don't talk back to me, boy." He stuck his thumbs in the front of his belt and poked out his chest. "I'm still on a killin' drunk." He came around to our side of the counter.

The smaller soldier smiled. "First the Injuns and then the niggers. Had to free 'em to kill 'em. Cain't be runnin' round destroyin' people's property."

Bubba formed a fist at his side, then let his fingers loose. He took a deep breath.

"Whoa," the big one said. "I think we're gitting us a rise outa of this nigger boy." He walked close and put his face just inches away from Bubba's.

176

Limbo backed up to the wall behind him and knocked a couple of cans to the floor.

"Hey, we don't want no trouble," I said.

"Shut up, nigger lover," he said.

"I ain't no such thing," I said.

"You with him?" the smaller barked at me.

"Yeah."

"Then you's a nigger lover," he said. "Seems right simple enough. You travel with a nigger, you a nigger lover. Ain't that right, Stu?"

The big one was staring at Bubba and didn't answer but nudged his face even closer to Bubba.

Bubba's eyes was unblinking.

"You wanna hit me, boy?" the soldier asked. "Go 'head, hit me."

Like lightning out of the dark sky over the desert, Bubba did. I swear I saw his fist push through to the back of the man's head. His face flattened and it hurt me just to watch it. My hand even ached from seeing it. And it was one of the most satisfying things I ever witnessed in my life. Immediately, though, the horror of it set in. The big soldier fell straight back, stiff as a tree.

The little soldier looked like he'd just seen a badger bite hold to his pecker. His mouth tried to make words but no sound came out. He looked over at me like he wanted me to explain something to him. Then he was fumbling with his gun in its holster. Bubba walked toward him with his fist formed and pulling back.

"Bubba," I said his name, trying to think of some reason why he should stop.

He didn't have to hit the second soldier, because the little guy passed out like a light. Bubba let down his hand.

Limbo leaned over the counter. "Mercy."

"Lordy doodle, Bubba," I said. "You have gone and done it now. You done killed government property. They gonna hang us both for sure."

"He ain't dead. Didn't hit him that hard." He looked at me. "Get the supplies so we can git out of here.

I turned my back to him and faced Limbo, shaking my head, saying, "What in the world is we gonna do now?"

"You two could shave yer heads and move west to Californy," Limbo said.

Bubba looked down at the soldiers, who actually seemed kinda peaceful stretched out like they was. "They don't even know who we are," he said.

"You ain't hard to find," I said. "You're the nigger."

"And any nigger will do," Bubba said.

He had a point.

Limbo said, "I'll tell 'em I heard you sayin' you was goin' south to Mexico."

"Much obliged," Bubba said.

"Thanks," I said.

Bubba went to the window and looked out. "I'm gonna go to Cahoots, and I'm gonna kill and scalp that Custer."

"Not that again. Bubba, that's just plain crazy," I complained. "You cain't fix nothin' by gittin' yerself shot full of lead." I turned to Limbo. "Ain't that just about the dizziest, most foolish notion you ever heard come out of a live man's mouth?"

23

THE WORLD CAME BACK to me in pieces, a flash of light here, a recollection there, Limbo's voice knifing in and fading out. Limbo's words twisted together into a rope that pulled me awake. He was singing a song, and none too well, I hasten to add. I unblurred my eyes and found the old-timer sitting in a rocking chair near the stove. I was lying on the floor with the soldiers. The big one was stripped down to his long johnnies. They was both still out cold.

"What in tarnation?" I shook my head.

"Your friend popped you on the bean. Hit you a good one," Limbo said.

I looked at the soldiers. "Why ain't they coming round?"

"He hit them harder," Limbo said. "He didn't hit you very hard, but it was a good one."

I stood over the little soldier. "He didn't even hit this fella."

"He went ahead and hit him after all. They ain't dead, though. If they was dead, I woulda moved 'em outside."

"Where's Bubba?"

"He put on that fella's uniform and said somethin' to hisself about killin' that—how did he put it?—that good-fer-nothin' government scum."

I rubbed my head. "And you didn't stop him."

"Cain't say that it crossed my mind to try."

The reward flashed across my brain. I had to stop Bubba before he got himself killed or else my fortune from turning in Sadie's abductors was lost. I looked at the soldiers again.

"How long will you let these boys stay tied up?" I asked Limbo.

"If'n you put 'em outside, I cain't say as I'd know they was there. Put 'em on the west side—I do my toilet on the east side."

"Thanks."

My head was aching something fierce. I kept feeling back there and checking my hand for blood or worse as I rode in the direction of that unpleasant little dung hole of a town. Damn that Bubba. Would I be able to stop him? He was mighty steamed up, and his hobby list of trangressions against white men was getting right healthy.

It was night when I got into town. I had to find that black man pronto, and I knew I had to keep myself from view of the sheriff. There was soldiers scattered all over the place, drinking, pissing against walls, grabbing women and shooting guns into the air. They was clustered in little groups. The hitching posts were lined full of horses. I walked my horse past a fight between a soldier and a regular cowpoke. I stopped another soldier.

"Where's the colonel?" I asked him.

"Oh, he's around," the man said, swaying from the effects of alcohol.

"You see him?"

"Yep."

180

"Where?"

"Around."

"When?"

"While ago."

The man was dang familiar. "Did you see him in the saloon?"

"Yep."

"Which one?"

"Yep."

"Where is Colonel Custer?" I pulled my gun and pointed it at him.

"You want to know where Colonel Custer is?" he asked, his eyes big.

"Yes!"

"The Colonel is in the Silver Dollar Saloon, upstairs, third door on the left, number four, with a yellow-haired woman in a purple dress and red stockings."

Before he was done, I'd spotted a figure on the roof of the Silver Dollar. Bubba.

"Now, git outa here," I told the soldier.

He ran.

I put my gun away and went into the alley and tied my horse next to Bubba's mule. I climbed up.

"Bubba," I whispered.

The figure paused in the shadows.

"Bubba."

"Go away."

"This is crazy." I was on the roof with him now. I shut up while a couple of fellas walked by. "Bubba, this don't make sense."

"It's the only thing that does make sense."

"You're gonna git yerself killed just as sure as a blind cat walks backwards."

"Prob'ly."

"What about yer land?" I asked him.

"What good is havin' land in this country?"

"Remember what you said? About stayin' there and shootin' anybody who come near? That was beautiful what you said. You could be an example to other ni– black folks."

He continued to crawl toward the middle window.

"Come on down."

"Afraid I cain't do that. I've gotta kill that bastard, kill him and scalp him just like he done to Big Elk."

"Wait," I said.

"Wait for what?"

I looked up and down the street again. The soldiers in sight were drunk enough not to matter none. "Let's talk about this thing."

He turned away and crawled closer to the window. "He's in there."

I moved up behind him and saw the yellow glow of a lantern inside.

"There's the whore," Bubba said. "Why, that's a man."

I looked in through the window over his shoulder. "Why, that's Custer. Why, he's wearin' ladies' unmistakables. Why is he doin' that?"

"Why, I don't know," Bubba said. "But it don't make no never mind. I come here to kill him, and that's the thing what's got to be done."

"Have pity, man. Look at him, gussied up like that. That there's a disturbed fella." The thought crossed my mind that he didn't look half bad.

"Awright, I'll tell him I like his bloomers while I slit his throat."

"Now, is that any way to be? A fella dressed like that cain't put up no fair fight," I told him.

"What is a fair fight, Marder?" Bubba asked.

"It just don't seem sportin', is all."

"This ain't sport." Bubba cast an eye to the street, then poised to bust through the window.

I put a hand on his shoulder and said, "Wait one second, Bubba."

"What is it?"

"Are you really gonna kill that poor man what's dressed like my departed mama, or are you just gonna give him a little bit of a scare?"

"If possible, I'll scare him to death. Failing that, I reckon I'll find some alternative method."

Then he reared back again, ready to spring forward through the window. I tried to hold on to him, and that turned out to be a fine bit of poor judgment on my part, because when the black man crashed through, I crashed through too, and there we both was on the floor looking up at Custer's curly locks capping a truly pitiful sight.

"What in the name of Caesar's army is going on here?" Custer demanded.

Bubba was on his feet quickly and stepping toward the man.

"What is your company, nigger?" Custer shouted. "Are you from the tenth?"

Bubba didn't say nothing.

"Answer me!" Then the colonel looked at me. "I know you," he said. "Tell me what's going on here."

Custer had his steely blues nailed to me when the first

183

blow found its mark. It landed on the right side of his face and turned his head so fast that his lips stayed put for a second. But he didn't fall, not right away. He stood there and his head clicked back around to center and then he fell straight back. His head bounced on the floor and actually served to wake him up.

The door opened and in stepped Loretta. "Oh, good Jesus in a tight toga!" she exclaimed, looking down at a head-shaking Custer with a robe hiked way up his hairy thighs.

"Loretta," I said.

"Look at him," she said.

"It was Bubba what hit him," I said.

"I mean, look at what he's wearin'." She closed and locked the door. "He's wearin' my robe and my lip paint." She kicked the colonel in his side, then seemed to regard me for the first time. "What the hell are you doin' here?"

"I'm with him."

Bubba was standing still as Congress, just staring at Custer, his fist opening and closing like a hawk's talons.

"Bubba's gonna kill this man," I told Loretta.

"He is?" She stepped over Custer and moved to stand behind me.

"What you waitin' for?" I asked Bubba.

"I'm waitin' for him to be able to feel the next one."

I was way deep into it now. So I pulled my gun from my holster and pointed the barrel at Bubba. He gave me a look that was brief and seemingly lacking in respect.

"Bubba, I'm afraid I'm gonna have to do my American duty and stop you and then turn you in as a nigger what's gone wild."

The spill through the window must have stunned my

184

reflexes, because the nigger snatched the pistol from me faster than beans go through a baby.

"Hey, that's mine!" I said.

He kept his gaze on Custer. He opened the chamber and let the bullets fall to the floor, then tossed the gun back to me.

"It's okay, Loretta," I said.

Custer came around a little more, his head rolling, his eyes trying to focus. He looked at each of us. "Of course, it would take three of you," he said. Then he seemed to remember just how he was dolled up. He pulled the robe down over his knees and rubbed his lips and looked at the red smears across the back of his hand. "What have you enemies of God's United States done to me? What kind of conspiracy is here afoot?" He pointed at me. "I should have suspected you from the beginning. Whoever you are." He looked at Loretta. "And you."

"I didn't have anything to do with this," she said.

"I suppose this isn't your robe," Custer said. Now his eyes were on Bubba. "And a nigger. After I fought to free all your kind."

Bubba leaned over and looked the man in his face. "What did you call me?"

"Nigger."

"What did you call Big Elk when you scalped him?"

Custer thought. "It was either red heathen or red dog. It was red something."

Bubba pulled back slowly and let loose a big black fist. Custer looked like a cow struck by lightning as he watched the knuckles fly toward his face. They landed almost silently and Custer lay on his back again, this time out cold.

"Damn," Bubba said. "He ain't worth the time killin' him would take."

"Hell, man," I said. "You gotta kill him now."

"You're right, Marder. He is pitiful. He ain't no more worth killin' than a snake what done already bit you."

"If'n you don't kill him, the army's gonna be after us for sure. You heard what he said. He's blamin' us all." I looked at Loretta. "It is your robe."

Loretta slapped me. "You got me into this. You were bad luck from the startin' gate." She slapped me again.

I felt lower than a pimple on a snake's ass. "You see why you gotta kill him, don't you, Bubba?"

Bubba offered Custer a last quick glance. "You want him dead, you kill him. Killin' is too good fer him. Leastways like this. Man like him oughta die in a special way, seeing it comin' and scared to death."

"What in the world are you talkin' about?" I asked.

Just then there was a knock at the door and a voice saying, "Colonel? Colonel? Everythin' awright in there?"

Loretta clutched to me and for a fleeting moment I loved it, and then I was back to being scared, right scared.

Bubba didn't say nothing. He just made his way across the room to the window and scooted through as easy as a lie falls from a preacher's lips. I tickled myself by actually thinking in my own personal brain, "That's for me." I got to the window and Loretta slugged me again because she wanted to go first.

Bubba was well out of sight by the time I was halfway through. The soldiers in the hall were laying shoulders to the door, and I let out a little scream which attracted the attention of the drunks in the street. The men laughed and pointed, soldiers and not, and rushed to help Loretta down

186

off the roof. I got down, too. The aroma of twenty intoxicated and unwashed men can form a right formidable wall and create a stifling blow to at least four of the senses. But I managed to get Loretta to my horse, on and riding with me out of town.

"Stop 'em! Stop 'em!" a man shouted behind us. "They done tried to kill the colonel by dressin' him up like a woman." Bullets began to fly, and we ducked as we galloped out of there.

By the light of the moon, I spotted Bubba's mule well in the distance. I was happy about the drunken state of them soldiers. If they was to find their horses, they sure as hell wouldn't be able to stay mounted, much less be able to locate and follow no trail. I hoped.

"I wish I could really tell you how much I hate you," Loretta shouted into my ear.

"You're doin' a right good job," I said.

"You are lower than devil spit. But I reckon you know that. You're a lizard made up to look like a sorry man. You're a lanced boil."

I tried to shut my ears by singing out a song. All I could recall was the first lines of "When Johnny Comes Marching Home." The "hurrah, hurrah" part was quite helpful, though.

Bubba was waiting for us about a mile away. Leastways he was not increasing the gap between us. I pulled us up beside him.

"We're in it now," I said. "I thought we was in it before, but that weren't nothin'. *Now* we're in it, and it feels just plain awful."

Bubba sighed and said, "I reckon you'd whine if they hung you with a new rope."

I considered that for a moment and said, "A bit."

"Those soldiers are goin' to be after us," Loretta said. "You good-for-nothin' maggot."

I smiled at Bubba. "She's takin' a shine to me."

"So I see," Bubba said.

"Where to?" I asked.

"The Indian camp," he said.

"Ain't nobody there what's alive," I complained.

"Yep."

"Yep? Yep to what?" I asked.

"Just yep," he said, and gave a look back in the direction of town.

"Indians?" Loretta said. "I cain't be goin' to be around no Indians. Have you heard what they do to white women? Why, the stories are plum awful. I shudder to even think about it. Those big braves in their paint, with their sweaty bodies and those loincloths and their long, straight, smooth, black hair falling over one shoulder just so."

Bubba looked at the woman. "You can stay here if'n you like." He paused for a moment. "You know, you're a right smart-lookin' woman, ain't no call to question that, but you ain't near enough to steer an Indian off'n his course. Me neither. But you're welcome to stay here and see how you fare with your own kind." With that, Bubba kicked his mule and rode away.

Loretta spoke into my ear. "You gonna let that nigger talk to me like that?"

"I reckon so," I said.

She punched me in my kidney. "Don't just sit here like a dang fool, follow the son of a bitch."

188

I rode back up to the black man's side. "Bubba, think about this. There ain't nobody at that village and there ain't nothin' there for us."

He paused his mule, but kept his eyes on the dark trail.

"Bubba, we need supplies and we need 'em bad. We got us a long ride comin' to who knows where. Man, the whole army is after us."

Loretta began to sob behind me.

Bubba looked at the sky. "I reckon what you say about the camp is true."

"Yeah, it is, and you know that goin' there will only make you feel low."

"So we beat word to the next town and git us some sundries."

"From there, maybe we should head west. Maybe to Californy, like that Limbo said."

Bubba started his mule and I followed. He bit off some chew, worked it and spit. "There goes my dream of ownin' land."

"A shame," I said.

"So, we're goin' to town?" Loretta asked.

"Yep," I said.

"Thank you, Jesus."

"But we's still wanted," I assured her.

She walloped me in the kidney again. "And to think I almost let you pay to sleep with me. There ain't enough money in the world. And here I am, clingin' to your miserable self in this god-forsaken country with some fluffy colonel out to see me dead 'cause I seen him wearin' *my* flimsies."

"You summed that up right nice, Loretta," I said. "It ain't

189

all that bad. The colonel ain't gonna git his hands on you. Not as long as I'm here."

"You need to stick your head up a horse's ass and take a deep breath. Maybe that'll wake you up." She slapped me across the top of the head. "I ain't gonna be with you long, you can count on that. As soon as we hit town, I'm away from you. You couldn't protect me from a one-legged hare caught in a trap."

I didn't say nothing.

"And you ain't gonna escape the army neither. They'll track you down and string you up fer sure."

I nodded. The possibility was more than distinct, it was downright imaginable—possible even. We were headed back to that dung hole of a town I called home. Wide Clyde and Taharry would be there, and as soon as word reached them about Custer, I wouldn't be no safer than a pat of butter on a fat man's plate.

"That nigger's crazy," Loretta said.

I didn't say nothing to that, but I did say, "I reckon you oughta reconsider lettin' me go."

"I ain't your woman. Lordy! Even if you was a man, I wouldn't be your woman."

"I know the folks in this town we're headed for and if'n you're wanted by the law, they'll snatch you up and drop you from the end of a rope faster'n anythin'."

She was silent.

"And there's no tellin' what all they'll do to you before they git around to lynchin' you."

"I ain't stayin' with you, that's all I know." She sniffed a little. "All my things are back there in Cahoots. My money. My clothes. I ain't got nothin'."

Money. I thought about money. Money was necessary.

190

Money was everything. Without it, I would be just like an Injun or a nigger. I had to have money. We were on the run. How far would they chase us? Maybe I'd have to run to Mexico. Money. The *reward*.

"Hey, Bubba," I called. "You know, we're gonna need us some money. Hell, we cain't even git supplies unless'n we got us some money."

"We'll git the supplies." He looked back at me. "We're outlaws now. I always been an outlaw. Now I know it."

24

WE WAS BEAT DOWN near dead by the time we clippity-clopped into town. Loretta was asleep but still mumbling about how much she hated my guts and how she couldn't wait to be rid of me forever. I really loved that about her, how she wouldn't let go of a thing. It was early morning and weren't nobody out except a couple of shopowners who was opening up. We turned off down a side street toward the livery just as I spied Jan Petersen sweeping his stoop. Loretta stirred behind me, then hit me.

"Would you leave off punchin' on me," I said.

"Where are we going?" she asked.

"The livery."

"That's just great."

"We can git some rest there."

"I don't want no rest. I just want to get away from you and your nigger friend."

And before I knew it, she was sliding off the back of my horse. Turning around in my saddle, I watched her trot back to the main street. I knew where she was going, though. The saloon. Where else would a saloon gal run? Dang, she was pretty.

I followed Bubba on to the livery and we dismounted and watered ourselves and the horses.

"Ain't this a fine now-you-done-it," I said.

"Yep."

"The whole army is after us."

"Yep."

"They'll hang us for sure if'n they catch us."

"Yep."

"Stop being so dang chatty and figger us a way outa this mess."

Bubba led his horse over to a mound of hay and, without looking at me, said, "I ain't figgerin' for no us. I'm figgerin' for me and me alone. You don't want to be with me. They'll find you for sure. 'There he is,' they'll say, 'the one with the nigger.'"

"That's a sterlin' point," I said, and the truth of it stunned me speechless as I watched him walk into the blacksmith shop.

"Bubba," I said, stepping into the building behind him. "Let's not split up just yet."

"Cain't say I see a reason not to."

"What about my Sadie?"

"I don't know your Sadie. Wouldn't know her if'n she was right here in front of me. Hell, man, you don't know her. You damn sure don't want her back."

"What about yer land."

Bubba was wandering around finding tools, hammer and pieces of iron and then he set to starting a fire.

"What you fixin' to do?" I asked.

"Put some shoes on my mule."

"The land, Bubba. I asked you about yer land."

"What land?"

194

"*Yer* land," I said.

"I ain't got no land. You ain't got no land."

"What're you talkin' about?"

"You lost it in a poker game. Leastways, I heard that." I searched for words.

"So, it's true. Cain't say I'm surprised. My mama didn't raise no stupid children."

"We'll need money, Bubba. Lots of money. We'll need it to git far away from here. We'll need it to eat."

Bubba was working the bellows and heating a length of iron. "*We* don't need a damn thin'. I'm gittin' out of here alone."

"There's a reward for them fellas what took my Sadie, the ones we's lookin' for. I saw the poster in the sheriff's office in Cahoots."

He didn't say nothing.

"It's five hundred dollars," I said.

"That ain't much money to git killed for," he said. He hammered the iron and it rang in my ears. "That's two-fifty for your life and two-fifty for mine. I know that mine's worth more."

"That's a lot of money," I said. "That's enough to carry us for a long spell."

He kept working.

"I'm gonna go get Loretta now, okay?"

"You do that."

"You wait here, okay?"

"I'm leavin' once I set my mule square."

"I'll be back in a hurry, so don't get all bent over with craziness and go tearin' outa here without me."

I could see that his project was going to take a while, so I left him there and made my way to the saloon.

Terkle the barkeep shook his head when I walked into his seedy establishment. He made a point of me seeing him move a bottle from the bar in front of him to the shelf behind. He looked right at me and said, "And all my life I believed buzzards ate the dead."

"Well, I ain't dead," I told him.

"Sure as hell cain't tell by lookin' at you, but I'm sorry to hear it nonetheless."

I looked around the tavern. It was pretty near empty, though there was evidence of a high time had by some. Taharry was sitting in the corner by the piany, his mouth wide open, kicked back in a chair, kinda awake, kinda asleep.

"Terk," I said.

"No."

"I ain't asked you nothin' yet."

"Don't matter none. The answer is no."

"What if'n I was to ask you if you wanted a dollar?"

"My answer would still be no. If'n you was to lay a dollar into my hand, I'd have to drop dead from unbelief."

"Anyway," I said. "You seen a pretty li'l gal come runnin' through here?"

"What you want her for?"

I leaned against the bar. "I cain't see where that's any o' yer beeswax."

"Well, I ain't sayin' if'n I seen her unless'n you tell me why for you want her."

"So, that's the way it is. Well, I ain't tellin' why I want her unless'n you pour me a glass of whiskey on the house."

Terk thought about that for a second or two, then put a glass in front of me. He grabbed the bottle from behind him and poured the drink. "Okay," he said. "Now, give."

I tossed back the shot and shook it off. "You see, I brung that li'l philly with me from Cahoots. Actually, she kinda followed me like a speckled pup. She was workin' in a tavern there, the Silver Dollar, to be presized, and she was makin' right fine money, but when she seen me she fell like a blind apple picker."

"So you're tellin' me that she's your woman."

"Yep."

"Well, cowpal, your woman came in here, took one gander at this fella what was countin' his winnings from a poker game that lasted all night and went upstairs with him." Terk smiled. "No doubty to tell him how much she loves *you*."

"Upstairs, you say?"

"Them stairs right there."

I looked.

"I reckon he didn't know she was your woman. He was a little fella."

"A little fella, you say."

"Right little, tiny even. Minuscule. A gnat."

"Don't that make the pig squeal," I said, shaking my head. "Well, I guess I'm gonna have to go up there and teach the little bug a lesson about handlin' other folk's handlin's."

I marched away from the bar toward the stairs and noticed that Taharry was more alert and heeding me some mind.

"There may be some blood spilt up there," I said as I passed by.

"Tano takiddin'."

Up at the top of the stairs, I paused at the first door. I listened through the wood and didn't hear nothing. I

197

squeezed the knob and gave it a twist. I stepped into the room to find Loretta stripped down to her lace bloomers and corset, sitting atop the little fella, rubbing his back.

"Aha!" I said.

My aha went for naught, as she didn't leave off for a second kneading his miserable flesh.

"AHA!" I tried again.

Loretta turned her head and seen me and screamed like I was a two-headed calf giving a sermon. She covered herself like I never seen her girlies before.

The fella turned over real slow-like and sat up. My first thought was, "He ain't that little." Maybe he had short legs, I thought. Then he unfolded himself and stood up to his full nine feet and twirled his mustache what was like raven wings nailed to his lip. He was butt naked and unashamed. He weren't really nine feet tall, but he was a good seven, well, maybe six, but he was a far cry from little. Loretta, covered now with the sheet, smiled evil at me and said, "Dirt, this here is Raleigh Dunnick."

"Ra-ra-ra-ra-raleigh Du-du-du-du-dunnick," I said. I knew the name well. He was the most villainous villain, the slimiest slime, the scummiest scum and the fastest gun in the territory.

Raleigh Dunnick grinned at me, a grin from hell, flashing white teeth that was uncommon in those parts. He said, "You done interrupted my carnal joy, boy."

"I'm sorry," I said.

"That slug's been a rash on my hindy quarters since I knowed he was alive," Loretta said. "Would you be kind enough to plug him into the hereafter, sugar?"

Raleigh Dunnick looked back at Loretta and said, "I'd

be happy to, delighted to, thrilled to comply and besides, I was gonna do it anyway."

I ran.

I reckon I prob'ly could have pulled my gun and shot him, but the thought didn't occur to me right off. My gentle nature, no doubt.

So, run I did, and a most remarkable thing followed and that thing was Raleigh Dunnick, who managed to find his pistol quickly and give chase. And he gave chase as naked as anything. I was at the doors to the street when I glanced back to see the horrible sight slapping down the stairs.

"Taoh tamy tagod."

Terkle just stood at his station behind the bar, drying a glass with a rag, shifting his gaze back and forth from Dunnick to me.

I ducked out into the street and ran like fire back toward the livery and Bubba. The black man was nailing a shoe to his mule's back hoof. He looked up as I come running but didn't pause from his task.

"We gotta git outa here," I panted.

"I reckon that ain't changed none."

"No, I mean for reasons anew," I said. "I done got myself into a whole heap of trouble. I done crossed trails with the gunslinger Raleigh Dunnick."

Bubba just whistled and shook his head.

"What we gonna do?"

Bubba looked past me down the alley. "*We* ain't gonna do nothin'."

I turned to see Raleigh Dunnick standing at the mouth of the alley, completely raw excepting for his gun belt. He held his hand away from his side and worked his fingers over his weapon. He stepped forward.

"I'm a-callin' you out," he said.

"Call me anythin' you like," I said. The livery was at a dead end and, I was afraid, so was I.

"Your time has come," Dunnick said.

"Dramatic cuss, ain't he," Bubba said.

"Bubba, help me."

But the nigger just led his mule to near the livery wall. He leaned there and looked on.

"Cain't we talk about this?" I asked.

"There'll be plenty of talkin' after you're dead."

He was no doubt right, but that talk was gonna lack a certain quality, namely me.

"Please, don't shoot me," I said.

"Son, I enjoy pathetic pleadin' as much as the next fella, but it don't hold no sway with me. And I'm worried about catchin' a chill out here. Now, let's git on with it. Make your play." He looked at Bubba. "Maybe yer nigger friend's got more guts than you."

Bubba pushed away from the hall and stood straight. "What did you call me?"

Dunnick was confused.

"I asked you what you called me."

"I think I called you a nigger."

Bubba widened his stance in the manner of the gunfighter.

"I ain't gonna participate in no fair fight with a nigger," Dunnick said.

"I'm ready any time you are," Bubba said.

I stepped out of the way.

Raleigh Dunnick moved first, and before I knew it both men had drawn and fired. Neither one moved for a long second, then Bubba slipped his pistol back into his holster.

Dunnick's gun remained raised and pointed at Bubba. The black man turned his back and started for his mule. It was the darnedest thing what ever I seen. And then Dunnick just fell face first into the dust.

"You killed him," I said.

"Yep," Bubba said. "That one, I killed."

"You killed Raleigh Dunnick. In a fair gunfight. Where'd you learn to shoot like that? In a fair fight. They gonna hang you for sure."

Bubba mounted his mule and gave a kick. "Good luck to you, Marder."

I watched him ride past the dead and naked Raleigh Dunnick. When Bubba was gone, I approached and stood over the fallen man. I felt cheated by the fact that he didn't have no pockets for me to rifle through. I took his fancy gun from his setting grip and was admiring the engraving on the handle when Wide Clyde and Terkle and Taharry showed up.

"Well, I'll be damned," Wide said.

"Tajesus tachrist."

They circled round me and Dunnick, whistling and scratching their heads.

"Well, dang it all," Terk said. "You killed Raleigh Dunnick. *The* Raliegh Dunnick."

"You're gonna be a legend," Wide said, then frowned with disgust. "You."

"Tawow."

"I'll say tawow," said Terkle. "I didn't know you had it in you, Marder."

"I reckon a man don't know what he can do till he sets his brain to starin' it in the face," I said.

"Imagine that, a butt-naked Raleigh Dunnick," Wide said. "Taharry, you'd best go get the undertaker."

So, there I was, sat down in the saloon with all the fellas around me, patting my back and buying me drinks and describing in great and glorious detail the gunfight betwixt me and the naked gunslinger. If I'd known killing a body carried with it that kind of treatment, I'd have done it long ago. Even Loretta had changed her tune from concentrated hatred to tolerant annoyance as she sat on my lap and stroked my face.

"I had to lure the varmint out into the street," I said. "I didn't want no innocent bystanders, especially you, Loretta, to be getting hurt or killed by errant lead."

"You sure looked scared when you run through here," Terkle said.

"Tayeah."

"He wouldn't have followed me if'n I hadn't looked scared."

"That sounds right," Joe Lucy said.

I looked around the crowd of high-stinking men. Aside from the three what come on the scene first, there was Joe Lucy, Roscoe Limpky, Josh Cutter and his oldest boy, Cheese.

"Weren't you just a teeny bit scared?" Roscoe Limky asked.

"What kinda man ain't a little scared?" Terk asked them all.

"I suppose I was," I admitted. "But I didn't have no time to be thinking on it." However, sitting there I did have time to consider Bubba, and I resolved never to call him a nigger again. He'd become right touchy.

Just then a cowpoke come busting in through the swinging saloon doors. "The army's a-comin'," he announced. "They says there are some traitors afoot what tried to kill some colonel by dressin' him up in female flimsies."

"Good Lord," Terk said.

"Imagine the indignity," said Wide.

Loretta looked at my eyes and whispered, "I still hate you with every ounce of my being, but get me the hell out of here."

I stood up. "Well, gents, this little lady and me is goin' out for a little stroll."

"A stroll?" they all said, then shared winks.

Then Wide scratched his smelly head. "Why you goin' out instead of up?"

"Tayeah."

"We just want us a little fresh air," I said.

Wide looked to the poke who'd just rode in with the news. "What do you know about them traitors?"

"There was three of 'em," the man said. "A woman one, a nigger one and a stupid one."

All eyes turned to me. I pulled my pilfered pistol of Raleigh Dunnick from my belt and pointed it smartly at the largest target in the room.

Wide said, "Don't nobody move funny."

"That's right," I said. "I done killed once."

Loretta was plastered to my side and we backed out of there. At the door, I said, "Don't nobody try to follow us. I'll put a hole in you for sure."

"Why'd you turn traitor, Marder?" Terk asked.

"I ain't no such thing," I said. "Now, everybody just stay quiet and calm-like and stay here. That's the important part. Stay here. I see anybody pokin' their business outside this door and pow."

Loretta and I fled the bar and ran to the livery. We collected my horse and stole one for her.

As we galloped out of town, I spied that preacher, Phrensie, and damn if he didn't have that child back with him again. She was all painted up and sad looking, sitting on the bench of his buckboard. I pulled up and gave a quick look back.

"What're you doin'?" Loretta asked.

"That there's little Jake," I said.

"Come on."

I kicked my horse and we made it out of there to the west, the sun in our faces.

25

IT WAS WHILE LORETTA was assuring me that as soon as
we was somewhere safe she was gonna do me fatal bodily
harm that I spotted a fire off in the dark night.

"Looky there," I said. "A fire. That could be Bubba."

"Who cares?" Loretta said.

"I hope it's Bubba."

"What you want with that darkie anyhows."

"He's gonna help me collect my money."

"You ain't got no money, and it won't do you no good
noways 'cause I'm gonna kill you soon."

I rode toward the fire.

Luckily, it was Bubba and not the three Yuk Yuks what
treated me so unkind. He was sitting there at the fire, staring at the flames. He didn't even offer up a look as we rode
into his camp. His back was to us. Loretta and I dismounted and sat with him to get warm.

We was quiet for a while or so, and then Loretta said
to Bubba, "I hate you, too." She looked at me. "But I hate
you more'n I hate him."

"Bubba," I said, "I need you to help me get that reward
money."

"I reckon you do, but that don't mean a hill of beans to me," he said.

"That preacher fella is back there in town." I paused and watched his face. "He's got that child back with him."

Bubba looked at me for the first time.

"And he's got her all dolled up like a little Kansas City whore."

"Hey," Loretta complained. "I'm a Kansas City whore."

"Nothin' personal," I said.

Bubba looked at Loretta and then stood up. "I reckon I oughta go git her."

Loretta looked at him like he was spitting out bullfrogs. "Wait, I don't understand. You mean to tell me you're goin' back into that town?"

"Bubba and me saved that little child from Phrensie once already, but somehow he done got her back. He's lookin' to sell her again."

She shook her head and talked to Bubba. "You're just gonna march your black behind in there and take a white girl from a white man?"

"Sounds ugly," Bubba said, "but yes."

"Why?" Loretta asked.

"That's what I keep askin' him," I said.

Bubba didn't say nothing.

"For a child," Loretta said, staring at the fire.

"He's crazy," I said.

"He's gonna git himself killed for sure," she said, and then looked at me. "Well, go with him."

"What?"

"I said for you to go with him."

"That's a dang fool idea," I said. I thought quickly that

if I helped Bubba, then he might help me. "Bubba, I'll help you if'n you go with me to git them outlaws."

"I don't need yer help," he told me.

"Well, how you plan to git her?" I asked.

"Just go in and git her, I reckon."

"That's just plain sewercide. You're a ni—a black man. They'll see you faster than a hog shits." Then I realized that if I was with him, I'd get caught, too. "Just let me go and do it," I said.

He stopped and looked at me. Loretta was staring at me as well.

"Let me do it. They'll spot you for sure, but maybe I can git in and out quietly and unseen-like."

"You'd do that?" he asked.

My heart was yelling no, but my head was counting that reward money. "Yes," I said. I was as confused as Bubba was. "But I'll be expectin' a favor in exchange."

Bubba nodded.

Loretta was near tears. "I guess I might have maybe had you figured all wrong, Dirt," she said.

"We all make mistakes, Doretta," I said.

"That's *Lo*-retta."

"And my name is *Curt*, if'n you don't mind." I was hoping she would offer to come and help, but instead she said, "I'll be a-waitin' for you right here."

My saddle was extra hard under my fanny bone as I headed back to that disgusting little hamlet. And the distance seemed too slight. The street was pretty calm. I tied my horse in an alley near the west edge of town and made my way through the shadows toward the saloon. I didn't know where to find the girl, but I figured Phrensie would be at the tavern. And there was his buckboard, parked and empty in the alley across from Terkle's place. I couldn't go in through the front door, because they'd catch me and sit on me until the soldiers came or just shoot me dead and have that be the end of it. I guessed that the preacher man was in one of the rooms upstairs, or at least the girl would be there.

I climbed the outside stairs to the side door of the saloon. I didn't have it in me to be on no more rooftops.

The door was unlocked and I slipped from the dark night into the dim glow of the empty hallway. I glanced down over the railing at the big open downstairs. The same fellas what was there earlier was still there, playing cards now and drinking. I didn't see Phrensie down there with them. I tippy-toed to the first door and wondered what in the world I was doin'. My ear to the door, I could hear a voice inside. I pulled my gun, my Raleigh Dunnick special, out of my holster, grabbed the knob, gave it a twist and pushed inside.

Phrensie was standing in the middle of the room, the lantern on full. He was holding a bible open in his hands and he looked up from reading, I guess. Jake was lying in the bed, covered to her neck with a sheet and blanket. Phrensie turned to me.

"You," he said. He looked at the gun. "What is the meaning of this?"

"I've come to take this here little girlie away with me."

"What is it about this child?" Phrensie asked.

"Beats the hell outa me," I said.

He looked at his bible. " 'And a child shall lead them.' But the book don't say who them is."

"Never you mind the theology, just let me have her and

208

we'll be on my way." I pulled back the hammer of the pistol.

"Hold your bladder, boy. Let's talk about this matter."

"Ain't nothin' to talk about."

"Why, sure there is." He closed the book. "Suppose I told you that this here child was possessed by the devil hisself."

"I'd say I believe you."

"I was just fixin' to exorcise the demons outa her when you so rashly interrupted. Just a few more words and the devil and his cronies would have been unleashed to visit another soul. Like yours perhaps."

"Now you shut up that noise."

"Just a few words more. Shall I say them? Spin spoon octaroon bill kill spill boom *bam!*"

"Hush," I told him.

"I kin feel Satan hisself liftin' from the child."

I looked at Jake and couldn't see no difference.

"Bill kill spill boom *bam!*"

And he startled me something awful, which normally wouldn't have mattered much to the man, but when I jumped, my finger pulled the trigger.

Phrensie fell to sitting on his butt and said, "She is free of Satan."

I didn't study on the bleeding preacher. I was too busy looking all around the room for them demons.

"The gun won't do you no good," Phrensie said. "The devil's on your shoulder."

I jumped again, slapping it away from me. Then I looked at the man and watched him fall back dead.

Jake threw back the covers and came running to me in a nightgown.

I stepped to the door and peeked outside at the empty hallway. If them men down there did hear the shot, they didn't care none. Somebody was banging on the piany.

I called to Jake, "Come on, let's go."

We stepped out of the room and I almost piddled my britches. The tavern was teeming with soldiers. I hurried Jake to the door, through the hallway, and out into the darkness. The streets, too, was lousy with army blue, and there I was, standing with a child in an over-big nightshirt and a painted face.

"What do we do?" Jake asked.

It was a good question but one I didn't want to hear right then, so I said, "Shut up." I looked around for a way out. "Back inside," I said.

We slipped back into the building and then back into the room, both of us wheezing with fear. The preacher was still dead.

"On the floor," I said.

Jake stretched out on the rug while I put on Phrensie's coat and hat. "Okay, I'm gonna roll you up in this here carpet." I did just that and hoisted the girl up and over my shoulder. I carried her out the door, down the hallway and to the outside. I walked down the stairs and to the street. I walked as close to the store fronts as possible, sticking to the shadows, pausing here and there to glance about.

"Hey!" a soldier called to me.

I stopped, my back to him.

"Where you goin' with that rug?"

"Rug?"

"Yeah, the one you're carryin'."

"Oh, this rug. Well, I'm the preacher in this here town and I gotta git this here rug over to my church right away."

210

"Why for?"

"Well, that's a long story that involves a lot of talkin' and you'd have to listen for just as long and you still prob'ly wouldn't understand it. Not because you ain't smart, but because you ain't a man of the cloth such as myself. Do you know the story of Jonah's coat?"

"Jonah's coat?"

"You see? We need the rug for a reinactment, 'cause we don't have the right kind of coat what's got no buttons."

"I don't understand."

"I told you that you wouldn't."

"Hey, don't I know you?"

"I hear that a lot. My mama told me I got that kind of face." Jake was getting heavy and I adjusted her on my shoulder.

"Is the rug heavy?"

"Naw, it's just the burden of my station, helpin' the downtrotted and the abjects of life."

The soldier nodded like he felt for me.

Somebody called to the soldier, and he turned away and walked to the voice. I ran down the next alley and out of sight. I rolled out the rug and got Jake on her feet. We scurried down the backs of the next buildings to my horse and we made it out of there.

Back where I left them, Bubba and Loretta was sitting by a small fire. Bubba held a couple of sticks in his hands. They wasn't talking none to each other then and I couldn't tell if they had talked at all, but I suspect they hadn't. Loretta stood as we rode into camp. Bubba looked up but didn't stand. Loretta saw Jake and came to help her down from my horse.

"She's awright, Bubba," I said.

"Awright?" Loretta held the girl's face in her hands and looked at it. "She's all painted. She's just a child."

"I told you that preacher man wanted to sell her into a life of you-know-whatty."

"Why, it's just awful," Loretta said. Loretta was sort of crying, like maybe she was seeing herself in a glass.

Jake stepped close to Bubba.

"You awright?" the black man asked.

Jake turned away from him without a word.

"Well, we got her back," I said. "Now what we gonna do with her?"

Loretta wiped the paint from Jake's face with the tail of the girl's nightgown. Then she wiped off her own face.

"You and this here woman gonna care for her, I reckon," Bubba said.

Loretta looked up.

"I'm sick of you tryin' to give me away," Jake said to Bubba.

"You ain't mine to give away," Bubba said.

"That's right," Jake said. "So you ain't had no right to give me to no Indians or to nobody."

"I reckon that's so, child," Bubba said. Then he looked at me. "You and me got business?"

"You mean the reward?"

Bubba nodded, then stood and faced Loretta. "You're a decent person. Take that horse and the girl and do what you think is right."

Loretta looked at Jake. She started to say something, but then stopped and nodded.

Bubba reached into his pocket and pulled out a small

212

roll of bills. "Take this here money," he said. "Git what you need."

Loretta took it.

"You had money?" I asked. "Why didn't you tell me you had some money?"

"Ain't your money."

26

WHAT WITH THE ENTIRE United States Army after me
and then having to watch my newfound love, Loretta, ride
away to the south with the child, it was a wonder my
stomach didn't just twist into a knot and kill me dead.

It was first light, and the dust of Loretta's leaving was
just settling. I hadn't slept a lick and my eyes burned. Bubba and me was mounted up and just starting out, pointed
toward the northwest and the red hills.

As we rode along, the clip-clopping of my horse and
Bubba's mule worked to make me sleepy, but I was jarred
awake with each step. I fought to keep my eyes open. I
looked at Bubba and said, "I do appreciate yer help."

He looked at me. "I said I'd help you."

"So, do you think we'll be able to keep from gittin'
caught by them soldiers?"

Bubba shrugged. "It would be a good thing."

"That Custer is a mean one. You know, he's got balls
the size of apples."

"What?"

"He's a tough one, is what I'm sayin'."

"You know a lot about him?"

"Just what I heard."

"He seemed to know you."

I cleared my throat. "Just seemed that way. The fool was delirious."

"I been studyin' on a question." Bubba spit tobacco juice to the ground between our rides. "How do you think them soldiers come to find Big Elk's camp?"

"Beats me."

Bubba grunted, his eyes forward.

"You think Loretta and Jake gonna be awright?"

"Cain't say. I reckon." Bubba looked at me. "What you gonna do when you git yer woman back?"

That was a dang good question that had been plum kicked out of my brain. She had slipped from my recollection, but now she was back. I wanted to be with Loretta. I wanted to get the money and then ride south to find her. Without the spread I wouldn't be needing no ranch wife.

The morning was crisp and clean as a bell on Sunday and there weren't no sign of soldiers. A couple of vultures circled above and I didn't like it none.

"You got any dreams, Marder?" Bubba asked out of the blue.

"Dreams?"

"Yeah, dreams."

"I got me some dreams."

"What do you dream for?" he asked.

I looked at the hills ahead of us. "I want me a lot of money and to be able to tell folks what to do and to have me a nice, big spread and to have my name mean somethin'."

He looked at me for the first time.

"What about you?" I asked.

He looked forward again. "All I want is one day where I ain't got to worry about a white man decidin' I looked crosswise at him, one day where I ain't got to worry just 'cause I hear a rider behind me, one day where I ain't called a boy."

"That ain't much of a dream," I said.

"Shame, ain't it." He leaned forward and scratched his mule's neck.

We rode on in silence. I had me a significant problem. Bubba was beside hisself. He'd already killed one white man and after he was done killing the vermin we was tracking, he'd be like a mad dog what's got a taste of blood. And the reward money. How was that gonna be split? Wouldn't be much, not all together. When all was done, I was gonna have to kill Bubba, shoot him dead. There was nothing else to do. Simple. And he was a nigger; I wouldn't have to cover it up, justify it or nothing.

We rode into the red-walled canyon. There was a pack of clouds casting shadows over things and it looked real spooky-like. Bubba paused and studied the terrain ahead.

"What is it?" I asked.

He pointed. "There's somebody up there."

"Where?" I strained my eyes to see. "I don't see nothin'. You mean up in them rocks?"

"I don't know for sure," he said. "I just know there's somebody up there."

"Is it them?"

"How the hell would I know?" He spit juice and glanced back behind us. "This here is a box canyon. If'n we go up there we'll come on 'em."

"Awright." I was nervous. "They seen us yet?"

Bubba shrugged.

"They'd be shootin' at us if'n they seen us, right?"

"How much did you say that reward was?" he asked.

"I think it was two hundred," I told him.

Bubba smiled a bit and it surprised me. He turned his mule around, looked at me for a long second and then started away from me.

"Where you goin'?" I asked.

"Just goin'."

"You cain't leave me here."

He turned in his saddle to look at me. "If them up there is your men, then they got the position and they got the numbers. I ain't dyin' for you. I ain't dyin' for nobody exceptin' myself." He turned away and started on.

I pulled my gun and fired into the ground in front of him, stopping him.

"Please, don't do that," he said without looking back. He kicked his mule again.

I had a good feeling about following him out of there, but I was scared, too. I was staring at him and I don't know what come over me, but it was like some kind of blind historical urge and that black man in front of me weren't no kind of real human being, just a thing. I raised my gun and put a bullet in his back.

Bubba fell off onto the dusty, red earth. Then he got up. And like nothing had happened, he climbed back atop his mule. I shot him again. Again he fell. Red dust floated all around him. His shirt was red with blood.

He got up and looked at me with a hawk's eyes, not the eyes of a man with two bullets in his back. I was into something frightening and my heart was standing still. He moved like he was taking a step toward me, but he stopped. He went back to his mule, grabbed the animal's back and pulled himself up. He hugged the mule's neck, reaching for the reins. I watched my finger, not the black man, as I squeezed off another round.

He didn't look at me this time. He struggled back onto his beast. I emptied my gun into him, the bullets producing little red clouds as they struck his dusty clothes. Finally, he was on his mule and turned to face me. I just sat there, my pistol empty. I thought I was a dead man.

He sat straight and fought with a deep breath. He looked at the sky and then at my eyes. A chill run over me and it seemed to me like a wind blowed through me. He pointed behind him out of the canyon and said—

"I'm goin' out there to make a life for myself somewhere. You done cheated me, lied to me and killed my brothers. I ain't got enough interest in you to kill you. But I'm goin' down there, like I said. And you or somebody what looks like you or thinks like you or is you will find me and you'll burn me out, shoot me or maybe lynch me. But you know something? You cain't kill me."

I watched him ride away.